Riley got up from his knees. "Man, Thorpe, you're some kinda lucky to live in a place like this."

"I guess you can call it luck. Right now, though, I'm half starving," said Thorpe, aiming a blatantly covetous eye at Riley's bag.

"Help yourself," said Riley. "So, how'd you find this cave?"

Thorpe gobbled a ham biscuit. "Crickets. I was looking in the hole at the other end of the tunnel and I heard crickets. They led me to the cave."

"What . . . do you like crickets?"

Thorpe set a bag of brownies to the side and jammed half a chicken sandwich into his mouth. "No. I don't like crickets. But if you get hungry enough, you'll eat anything."

"Yuck!" Riley was repulsed. "You eat crickets?"

Thorpe shot Riley a condemning look. "You sure ask a lot of questions for someone who just had his life saved."

"Sorry."

Thorpe devoured the other half of the sandwich. "You gotta excuse me if I'm a little snappy. I've been on the lam for a while and I'm not used to being around people."

ALSO AVAILABLE IN LAUREL-LEAF BOOKS:

It's Nothing to a Mountain

Sid Hite

Published by
Bantam Doubleday Dell Books for Young Readers
a division of
Bantam Doubleday Dell Publishing Group, Inc.
1540 Broadway
New York, New York 10036

ISBN: 0-440-21945-0

Reprinted by arrangement with Henry Holt and Company, Inc.

Printed in the United States of America

November 1995

10   9   8   7   6   5   4   3   2   1

OPM

For my brother

It's Nothing
to a Mountain

Part One

From this valley they say you are going,
We will miss your bright eyes and sweet smile.
For they say you are taking the sunshine
That brightens our pathway awhile.

—"THE RED RIVER VALLEY,"
POPULAR FOLK SONG

One

—

Long, long ago ... somewhere in the vicinity of four hundred million years ago ... at a time when plants were just beginning to leave the sea and live on land ... the continental plate of North America collided with the continental plate of Eurasia. It is nearly impossible for a human to conceive the immense pressure these two merging land masses exerted upon each other. Even with megatons as a unit of measure, one would not begin to approach an understanding of the thrust brought to bear in that conflict. Yet that was just for geological starters; at some point during the next hundred and fifty million years, the continental plate of Africa drifted over and joined the assembly. With this additional force, the continents buckled, thrust upward at the edges, and gave birth to the Appalachian chain of mountains.

During the next hundred and fifty million years (plus or minus thirty million years), the continents began to drift apart, leaving the Appalachians behind on what is now the eastern seaboard of North America. Once they were grand mountains, lording over the world like towering giants, but today, after an aeon of weathering, they are childlike when compared with the earth's newer creations, such as the Alps, the Andes, or the Himalayas.

Beginning in Virginia and extending south into North Carolina is a section of the Appalachians known as the Blue Ridge Mountains. They are lucky hills. Not only were they spared the glacial projections of the last ice age, but they also never suffered the marring fury of a volcanic eruption. Shaped instead by the relatively gentle hand of wind and rain, the Blue Ridge are not only the oldest mountains in the world, but they are also the most beautiful. (You may dispute this claim if you wish, yet you do so in vain.)

How can a human being, who with luck might live a century, fathom the concept of a hundred million years of maturity? How can a Homo sapiens sapiens, who as a species only evolved a brief forty thousand years ago, begin to imagine the character of a mountain? We are upstarts. We just arrived. Forty thousand years might impress a poet, but it is nothing to a mountain.

• • •

Much, much more recently, a large brick house was built atop a narrow, fingerlike plateau in the Blue Ridge Mountains of Virginia. Three hundred yards wide at its base, it arose out of the beautiful and fertile Sparkling River Valley. At an elevation of nineteen hundred feet above sea level, the plateau softened into a relatively flat plane. Here the house was built. At the west end of the plane were rock-faced cliffs that dove sharply into a deep, wooded canyon. On the far side of the canyon in the west, rising stolidly into the sky, was a razorback mountain called Bluff Top Ridge.

The brick home atop the plateau was called the Upper Place. It was constructed soon after the end of the Civil War by two male descendants of Rufus Julius Sutter. The property, once more than seven thousand acres, had been granted to Rufus in 1791 by the United States government. It was his reward for services rendered during the Revolutionary War. He had been a scout, which in those days called for a spot of spying as well. He must have been a rather hale individual, because according to Sutter family legend, he somehow survived the killing winter of 1778–79 at Valley Forge, Pennsylvania. The Sutter legend also holds (though no documents remain to prove it) that Rufus knew and reported directly to General George Washington. Whether Rufus actually knew the young general is a moot point as far as this story goes. What matters is that the grant included all the land east to west between the Sparkling River and Bluff Top Ridge, and north to south from Gallihugh Mountain to Jagged Gap.

One hundred and seventy-eight years after Rufus's reception of the deed, on a windy April afternoon in 1969, his great-great-great-great-granddaughter, fourteen-year-old Lisette Sutter, sat crying on a bench in an ornamental garden at the Upper Place. She was small for her age, with dark hair, big brown eyes, and large ears. Occasionally she was called Miss Mousey, but not today. Today she was more like a lioness roaring in pain. The week before, her mother and father, Alison and Russel Sutter, had been riding in a car that crashed through a guardrail, plummeted into a gulley, and burst into flames.

After the double funeral of her parents, Lisette and her twelve-year-old brother, Riley, were moved from their natal home in the Sparkling River Valley and installed at the Upper Place with their paternal grandparents, Clara and Preston Sutter.

The ornamental garden where Lisette sat crying had been designed by her great-great-grandmother. It was surrounded by six-foot-high, dry-set granite walls, which afforded both wind protection and privacy from the house. The walls were covered with various lichens and mosses, and also served as a hunting ground for Fence Swift lizards, Fowler toads, and the occasional black snake. Outside of the south and east walls were a variety of fruit trees, which cast a rotating shade over the garden in summer. In the center of the space was a reflecting pool fed by underground pipes connected to gutter downspouts on the house. Any overflow drained through a spoke wheel of irrigation canals.

The bench upon which Lisette sat crying had been hewn in 1931, by her grandfather, Preston Sutter. It was made of American chestnut, which had died profusely in that year of blight.

Lisette cried and cried. Except for a few short periods of fitful sleep, she had been crying day and night since hearing the news of her parents' demise. They were the first people she had ever known to die, and the pain of that horrifying loss did not seem to be diminishing with time. It was as if the whole universe were being sucked into a bottomless black hole. For all Lisette felt and knew at the moment, she might continue to cry for the rest of her life.

Compounding Lisette's grief was her confusion at a thought her grandmother, Clara Sutter, had introduced after the funeral. Clara, usually so sweet and gentle, had surprised Lisette with her angry intolerance of the facts. She had waited until they were driving home from the cemetery, then lifted her dark veil and turned to the backseat of Preston's big Buick, where Lisette sat crying beside her bewildered Riley. In a voice heavy with her own pain, yet clear in its delivery, Clara informed her grandchildren, "I know you heard the preacher say God works in mysterious ways, and that it was not for us here on earth to judge God's deeds, but I want both of you to understand that your Pa-Preston and I don't ever intend to forgive God for what happened to your mom and dad. Russel was our son, and Alison was his wife, and there have never lived any people who were more decent. God made a mistake in taking them."

Lisette had always been confused about God, and now she was even more so. Yet she did understand the meaning of death. Or at least she knew what it meant for her. Never again would she see her mother's flashing smile, or feel the sheltering embrace of her father's arms. Gone from this world was her mother's fine, lyrical voice. Gone was her father's hearty laugh. Lisette knew without hope that she could never again sneak to the river, peer from behind a tree, and catch the two of them smooching.

She cried on . . . and soon she recalled another thought, also introduced on the day of the funeral. This one had been presented by her precocious younger brother. He had waited until the undertaker's stooped assistant began shoveling red clay into the open grave, then turned and whispered in her ear, "Lisette, if heaven really does exist, and if half of what they say about the place is true, then Mom and Dad are going to be all right. It's you and me who have to keep on living. If we're ever going to be happy again, we better send them into the past and learn to live in the future."

As Lisette was pondering Riley's advice, she heard footsteps approaching along the gravel path. They were followed by the scratchy sound of her grandfather's voice. "Is there crying out here, too?"

Lisette took a deep breath, wiped the tears from her cheeks, and announced with a sniffle, "Come, Pa-Preston. I'll stop."

Preston sat on the enduring old bench and put an arm over Lisette's shoulder. It was evident from the redness in his eyes that he too had recently been crying. Lisette's grief suddenly subsided and was replaced by an urge to comfort her grandfather. She lay her head against his chest and sighed. After a long, silent pause, he coughed and inquired, "Seen Riley?"

"Not since breakfast."

Preston's chest rose and fell heavily. "That little devil. I've got the feeling he never listened to what I said."

"Oh, he never listens," Lisette said matter-of-factly.

"Dad used to say he was convinced that Riley's ears were broken."

Preston snorted. "I'll break more than his ears if I find out he didn't mind what I told him."

Bluff Top Ridge and the land immediately to the west of the Upper Place were part of a sixteen-thousand-acre tract of forest managed by the Virginia State Park Service, all of which was in timber reserve. South and west of the park land was a forty-eight-hundred-acre parcel owned by the Stills Bend Hunt Club. The club was a mostly defunct organization, comprised of aging men who had slowly grown weary of blood sports. They kept the property for its ramshackle lodge, which they sometimes used for poker games or drinking binges. North of the club were nineteen hundred acres belonging to the retired Judge Applegate and his wife, Phyllis. The combination of the aforementioned tracts of land and the Sutter property on the east side of the ridge created a swath of nearly thirty thousand acres of undeveloped mountain woodland. A very large patch of woods.

Earlier that day, completely ignoring his grandfather's edict that he not leave the vicinity of the Upper Place, Riley had gathered together his camping gear and headed into the vast forest. He did not enjoy disobeying his grandfather, but that morning he had reached the point where he just had to get away from the steady stream of neighbors who stopped by the house to offer their condolences. It is one thing to feel hurt in your own heart, but something else to see it in the faces of everyone around you. Riley honestly thought he would explode if he had to witness one more grown man standing in the den with his head bowed, his hands trembling, and his posture belittled by grief.

Having grown up in the Sparkling River Valley, Riley had always been aware of Bluff Top Ridge looming in the distance. For him it was an abstract, faraway place in the west where his thoughts would sometimes run at sunset. Until today, he had never really considered making a journey there.

It was not an easy trip. It took him two hours to descend the cliffs beyond the house and find his way across the canyon. It took another hour to scratch and scramble up to the lowest point atop the north end of the ridge. His progress was somewhat encumbered by the pup tent, blanket, and sidebag he carried, but there was never any question of leaving these behind. The bag was filled with choice selections from the numerous food offerings that had been arriving at the Upper Place since the day after Alison and Russel Sutter left this world.

As Riley followed the lay of the ridge southward

toward the summit, he was greeted by an increasingly stiff wind. Only because he was an incisive and sure-footed lad did he cover the distance in twenty minutes. When he arrived at the boulders marking the highest peak, he threw his gear on a table of flat rock and stood admiring the sweeping view. All around, spring was painting the treetops a soft green. To the west were the sprawling woodlands of Broken Valley. In the south the Sparkling River cut through the gorge at Jagged Gap. To the east was the undulating expanse of the Sparkling River Valley. As Riley gazed out over the world, he was filled with a kind of satisfying awe. For the moment, at least, he had escaped the darkness of death's company.

While Riley admired the scenic vista, the brisk April wind gusted across the top of the ridge and snatched his favorite baseball cap from his head. With the quick reaction of a star shortstop, he grabbed for the cap. He missed. The cap skipped across the flat rock, slapped at a boulder, then sailed into the west. He started to chase it, but when he reached the shoulder of the ridge and glanced into the chasm where the cap had disappeared, he quickly accepted that it was gone forever.

Riley returned to the flat rock beside the cluster of boulders marking the tip-top of the ridge. He intended to climb them, but he wisely decided to wait and do so after the wind died down. (He was brave but not stupid. Although Russel had believed his son's ears were broken, Riley had been listening when he said, "There is very little difference between courageousness and foolishness if you do something that breaks your bones.") Riley glanced up at the top boulder and thought, I'll get to you in a minute, then turned to the task of erecting his tent. As he squatted over the canvass bundle and released the binding rope, the already-stiff wind increased in velocity and began to whip over the ridge at near-gale force. He knelt on one corner of the tent and began to unfold it on the flat rock. The more he spread out the canvass, the more the wind grabbed and pulled at his portable shelter. Using both knees, an elbow, a forearm, and his chin, he finally managed to stretch the tent into a vaguely square shape. This was progress, except now he was spread eagle on the tent without any appendages free to reach the rope he needed to secure the tent to the rock. After pausing to visualize the coming act, he exercised his only option. One . . . two . . . three . . . he rolled as rapidly as he could and reached for the rope. He was quick, but the wind was quicker. It surged under the canvass and lifted it with a violent flutter. He dropped the rope and lunged for the tent, just barely managing to grab a corner loop. The whole contraption popped open, filled out like a balloon, and began to tug him westward. He set his heels and leaned backward. What happened next happened fast. By the time he realized he was airborne, his feet were dangling high over the chasm where his cap had flown. "Sheeeeeeit!" he hollered.

Providence was with him. Twelve seconds and forty yards later he crashed into the top of a large spruce tree. Branches snapped and he careened forward. Somehow he held on to the tent, which snagged the broken treetop and ended his fall. His only problem now was that he was stuck with his arms extended over his head, his back resting upon splayed branches, and his feet dangling twenty yards above the rocky slope below.

His mind had just begun to clear and review the situation when he heard someone snicker, "Now, that was a nifty maneuver."

Riley looked down and saw a skinny, barefoot boy dressed in tattered trousers, a soiled T-shirt, and a very familiar-looking baseball cap. The kid looked up and grinned. With a flash of intuition, Riley knew he was staring down at the Greenwood kid who had been missing from High County for almost a year.

"I always wondered if it was possible to fly a tent." The boy slapped his thighs and laughed sarcastically. "I reckon you're surprised you're still alive?"

"Yeah," Riley replied weakly.

"Good feeling, isn't it?" The boy bobbed from one bare foot to another. "Don't believe I'd trade being alive for anything."

"No," Riley agreed wanly. His shoulders and arms ached, and his hands burned painfully where the loop was cutting into his wrists. All of his senses informed him that a fall would break his legs.

The boy on the ground shrugged and rolled his eyes as if he knew he was about to be inconvenienced. "Let me guess. You're going to ask me to help you get down from there."

"If you wouldn't mind," Riley said meekly.

The Greenwood kid smirked and sat down. He glanced casually at his hands, turned to inspect the woods behind him, then peered thoughtfully back at Riley. It was obvious he was weighing his options.

"I can't hold on forever."

"Don't suppose you can." The boy chuckled. Still he did not move.

After a long minute (it felt like ten to Riley), the boy stood up and mused aloud, "Let me see. I could leave now and forget all about you. But you've already seen me. And that's a problem. I could wait until you fall, then leave you for dead. Or, I suppose, there is the possibility I could help you."

"Please help." Riley sounded as though he might

cry. He did not think he had the strength to hold on much longer.

"Hey, I won't leave you for dead. That was a joke. What's your name?"

"Riley Sutter. I'm from the valley."

"I know where the Sutters are from."

A branch cracked. Riley braced himself for a fall that did not come.

"I tell you what," said the boy on the ground. "If you'll swear you never saw me, then I'll consider helping you down."

"I won't tell a soul about you," Riley blurted.

"I said swear you never saw me," barked the Greenwood boy. "I am not here. You got that? I don't exist."

"Okay. I swear you're not there," Riley hollered. "I swear. I never even saw you earlier."

The boy on the ground cracked a thin smile. "Guess I'll have to take your word on that. You even sounded like you meant it."

"I did," Riley groaned. "Could you hurry?"

"I'm coming," snickered the Greenwood kid. Then he darted forward, shimmied up the tree trunk, lifted himself onto a lower branch, and climbed to Riley's rescue.

Two

The April night was moonless as Clara Sutter sat in her rocker on the front porch of the Upper Place, silently regarding her husband, Preston. Together they were waiting for Riley to return home. Lisette, finally worn out from crying, had gone to bed early. Although Clara was concerned about her errant grandson, her real worry was for Preston. He was no longer the young fellow she had married, and tonight she feared for his heart. The poor muscle had nearly broken when he learned that his son and daughter-in-law had been abruptly taken from this world.

As Clara watched, Preston fidgeted. He was wrestling with ambivalence toward Riley. On the one hand he was disappointed that the boy had gone against his word, yet on the other, he admired the rascal's gumption. In Preston's view, gumption was a cardinal virtue, and of that, it was clear Riley had been richly endowed. Preston knew he was not a bad kid, just a rambunctious one with a slight discipline problem. Indeed, in the present circumstances, he could empathize. During the past week, he too had longed to get away from the house and walk alone in the mountains. This time, he decided, he would forgive Riley. Later, he figured, he would instruct the boy in some definite rules of conduct.

While Preston fidgeted, Riley was deep in the mountains, enjoying one of the more fascinating nights of his young life. He had chosen not to reflect on the distress he might be causing at the Upper Place, and was concentrating instead on the manner and words of his new friend, Thorpe Greenwood.

After retrieving Riley's gear, Thorpe had led him north along the ridge, then east past the canyon to a series of small hills located in the woods near Gallihugh Mountain. Concealed halfway up one of the hills was the entrance to Thorpe's residence. To enter, it was necessary to penetrate a dense thicket of mountain laurel, climb onto a rock ledge, drop into a hole, squat, then snake forward through a ten-foot tunnel. At the end of this blind passage was an angled shaft that opened upward into the hidden chamber that Thorpe called home.

• • •

Some three to four hundred million years ago, when the Appalachian chain was buckled into existence, shelves of ancient, multibillion-year-old Precambrian rock were crushed and mixed with relatively new sedimentary deposits thrown up from the ocean floor. In the process, countless pockets of calcium carbonate (coral, seashells, and silt) were captured within large folds of this mixed rock. Through time the carbonates turned to limestone, and in those instances where water found the limestone—either trickling down from surface streams or welling up through the aquifer—the deposits dissolved and formed what geologists call solution caves.

"You can stand," Thorpe told Riley as he popped through the open shaft and entered the stone chamber. "But don't move until I get some light in here."

"I won't." Riley was glad to obey. He could hear crickets chirping as Thorpe rustled around the cave. They fell sharply silent when Thorpe struck a match and ignited a pile of kindling wood. As the darkness fled into remote crevices of the space, Riley was astonished to find himself standing in a cone-shaped room, at least twenty feet in diameter. To his left was a twisted stalactite reaching to within inches of the stone floor. Overhead was a craggy, soot-stained ceiling.

"Holy Jupiter," exclaimed Riley. "This is absolutely fantastic!"

Thorpe shrugged. "It's all right . . . for a small cave."

"Small?"

"I know a couple bigger ones."

Riley drank in the details. Stacked neatly against the wall to his left was a rick of firewood. Placed orderly on top of the wood were the principal articles of Thorpe's solitary life: extra clothes, blankets, pots, pans, candles, flashlights, canned food, dishes, a bucket, tools, a slingshot, rope, books, magazines, pens, and paper. Here and there, set randomly in cracks and on natural shelves, was a collection of found baubles: turtle shells, hawk feathers, deer antlers, snakeskins, a fox skull, a raccoon tail, and one exceptionally large, dried tree fungi.

A chrome spaceship would not have interested Riley more than the interior of Thorpe's cave. Smoke from the fire spiraled up into a sooty fissure at the apex of the ceiling. The stone floor on which he stood sloped gradually away from the entrance and dropped beneath a gap at the base of the far wall. The gap looked like a frowning mouth. It was about eight inches high in the middle and it tapered evenly toward the corners. With the charred end of a burned stick, Thorpe had artfully added lips, a mustache, a proud nose, dramatic eyes, and a wrinkled brow. Riley crossed the cave and stood in front of the face. After a moment he got down on his knees and attempted to peer inside the mouth. He was startled by a rush of damp air. "It's breathing."

Thorpe acknowledged him with a nod. "Good thing. The whole place would fill up with carbon monoxide if it didn't."

"Wow. Ventilation."

"I think there's a huge cavern down in there."

"You do?"

"Feel how moist the air is. The way I figure it, there must be an underground stream or a lake at the bottom."

"Have you gotten in there?" Riley asked excitedly. "I bet I could fit."

"I've stuck my head in and looked around with a flashlight. It drops straight down."

Riley got up from his knees. "Man, Thorpe, you're some kinda lucky to live in a place like this."

"I guess you can call it luck. Right now, though, I'm half starving," said Thorpe, aiming a blatantly covetous eye at Riley's bag.

"Help yourself," said Riley as he turned back to the face. "Is that someone you know?"

"Just a picture."

"So, how'd you find this cave?"

Thorpe gobbled a ham biscuit. "Crickets. I was looking in the hole at the other end of the tunnel and I heard crickets. They led me to the cave."

"What . . . do you like crickets?"

Thorpe set a bag of brownies to the side and jammed half a chicken sandwich into his mouth. "No. I don't like crickets. But if you get hungry enough, you'll eat anything."

"Yuck!" Riley was repulsed. "You eat crickets?"

Thorpe shot Riley a condemning look. "You sure ask a lot of questions for someone who just had his life saved."

"Sorry."

Thorpe devoured the other half of the sandwich. "You gotta excuse me if I'm a little snappy. I've been on the lam for a while and I'm not used to being around people."

Riley nodded that he understood. Quietly, he moved to sit by the fire and study his host. Thorpe had the bluest eyes he had ever seen. He also had a head full of extremely tangled black hair. There was something about the way he greedily stuffed food in his mouth that made Riley wonder if he was dangerous. He hoped not; it was obvious that the older, larger Thorpe would easily best him in a struggle. He had a kind of no-nonsense, this-is-not-a-game air about him.

Thorpe Greenwood may have eaten crickets, and he may have looked a mess, but he was no one's fool. Indeed, for someone only fifteen years old, he was uniquely shrewd and resourceful. His situation, of course, had forced him to develop his thinking skills. For ten months now he had been living on his own in the shadows of Bluff Top Ridge, and there was little about his life that came easily. Survival was the main theme of his daily and nightly existence.

When Thorpe first entered the mountains after the disturbing events that drove him from his home, he bivouacked in a ravine near Jagged Gap. Then later, after stumbling upon the hidden cave, he moved his stockpile of supplies and set up a permanent home. In the three hundred days he had been on the lam, he had seen many people—campers, hunters, hikers, and the residents of the homes he sometimes robbed—but Riley was the first person to whom he had spoken.

He gobbled another ham biscuit, wolfed down two brownies, then hoisted a jug of water and gulped. Afterward he burped and declared, "I forgot how much fun it was to eat."

"I could have brought tons more food," said Riley, eager to ingratiate himself with his host. "The house is full of food."

"It is?"

"Yeah. My parents died last week, and it seems like the whole valley has been cooking and bringing us stuff."

Thorpe nodded thoughtfully. "That must have been the big funeral I saw a few days ago up on Gallihugh Mountain."

"That was them." Riley sighed, hit by a wave of sorrow.

"Pretty popular, weren't they?"

"Yeah," acknowledged Riley. "Everyone liked Mom and Dad."

As much out of curiosity as to end the awkward pause that had settled over the cave, Thorpe inquired, "What happened?"

"Car accident." Riley's shoulders slumped. Then in a sudden rush of words he explained. "Their car went through a guardrail. Then it crashed in a gulley and caught on fire. The only good part, if you can call it good, is they were probably dead before they burnt up. At least that's what Pa-Preston said."

"Jeez," Thorpe exclaimed. Slowly, ponderously, he turned and reached into a cloth satchel hanging on the wall behind him. From it he withdrew a pipe and a pouch. "You must feel pretty rotten."

Riley stifled a cry.

Thorpe packed the rosewood bowl of his pipe with tobacco. He took a stick from the fire, and then before putting the burning end of it to the bowl and puffing, he asked, "How old are you?"

"Twelve. I'll be thirteen in August."

Thorpe drew on the pipe and stared thoughtfully at the fire. After blowing a couple of smoke rings toward the ceiling, he mused sagaciously, "You know, Riley, after twelve, a guy doesn't really need parents."

"I hadn't thought of that."

Smoke streamed from Thorpe's nostrils. "That's only my opinion, of course."

Riley nodded thoughtfully, then pointed to the pipe and asked, "Where'd you get that?"

"Oh, this." Thorpe shrugged. "I took it from the lodge up at the hunt club. Not that I'm proud of stealing, or anything. I'm not. I only do it because it has to be done, you understand. A man must have supplies."

"Gotta have supplies," Riley agreed.

Excepting those individuals with claustrophobia, there is something inordinately calming about sitting inside a cave by a fire. Somehow, one feels safely removed from the threats of the world. Perhaps this feeling comes to us from our not-so-distant, cave-dwelling ancestors. Perhaps it is a product of the elements. For whatever reason, Riley soon began to feel deeply relaxed and reassured by the situation. During the speechless interlude that settled over the cave, he found the mental leisure to review the recent, dramatic changes in his life. In the past eight days, he had lost his parents, been moved to the Upper Place, and was now making friends with a fugitive who lived in a hidden cave and smoked a stolen pipe. The latest development was clearly the most promising of the lot.

Riley tried to recall what he knew about his host. Somewhere in the back of his mind was a memory of his mother and father discussing the boy who had disappeared from High County. There had been something unusual about the story ... something strange, but he could not recall the details. Vaguely, though, he seemed to remember that Thorpe had been a victim of certain circumstances.

Riley was drawn abruptly from his reveries when he looked over and noticed Thorpe gazing intently in his direction. There was a quality to the gaze that caused Riley's feeling of security to flee. It was a hard look, almost threatening. When Thorpe's voice punctured the silence, his words did nothing to allay Riley's fears. "You should know that I'm not leaving these mountains anytime soon. So that means I either trust you to keep your trap shut, or I have to eliminate your ability to speak."

Riley threw an involuntary glance toward the exit hole and mumbled sheepishly, "I won't say a word."

Thorpe set his pipe aside, then reached into a pocket and withdrew a six-inch folding knife.

Riley became suddenly aware of the heat from the fire. He tried to swallow but his mouth was too dry.

"It doesn't matter to me why," Thorpe continued in a grave tone. "Or how. Or whatever you might think of—I don't care if I belly up and die of rot—but you have to swear that you'll never, ever dream of telling a soul you even think I live anywhere near Bluff County."

Riley put a hand over his pounding heart. "I swear, Thorpe. Even if someone put a gun to my head, I wouldn't admit I'd ever heard of you."

Thorpe flicked the blade from its sheath. "I don't believe in common swears. They don't mean much."

"They don't?"

"Nope." Thorpe shaved a few hairs from his forearm. "Even being friends isn't really enough of a reason to trust somebody completely."

"It isn't?"

"Nope."

"S-s-orry," Riley stammered. "But who . . . ca-can you trust?"

Thorpe's blue eyes flashed with devilish amusement. "A blood brother, Riley. You can always trust a blood brother."

It took a second for Riley to comprehend what

Thorpe was suggesting. Then, with a great sigh of relief and much cheer in his voice, he concurred, "Oh, yeah. Definitely. You can trust a blood brother."

"Glad you agree," Thorpe snickered. "Now roll up your sleeve and give me your left arm."

Riley cringed. "My left one?"

Three

Early on Sunday morning, Lisette was awoken by a dancing of light in the east window of her newly adopted bedroom. It was a top-floor, corner room, with slanted ceilings and a rose motif wallpaper. She loved the space. It had always been her favorite place to play when she visited her grandparents. Clara had known this, and as soon as the decision was made to move the children to the Upper Place, she had prepared the room for Lisette.

Lisette blinked at the morning rays and propped herself up in bed. Subconsciously, her fond familiarity with the room was easing the trauma of her transition. (Such is the human psyche that persons who have suffered great loss should find solace in those places and things that have not changed.) The simple knowledge that during the next rainstorm the

slate roof above would resound with the rat-a-tat-tat
of a million paper drums was a source of great reassur-
ance for her. It bolstered her spirits to know that she
could cross to the south window and look down into
the walled garden at the reflecting pool, or go instead
to the east window and gaze out over the valley,
where the Sparkling River shimmered snakelike on
its journey to the sea.

As Lisette studied the light, she formulated her
first thought of the day. It was a question, which gave
birth to a string of questions. How, Riley? How do
we send Mom and Dad into the past? And how do we
learn to live in the future? If they are in heaven and
we are on earth, isn't that all at the same time? Is the
past just a place where we put things that hurt, and
the future a place where we look to be happy?

If the soul has eternal life, she reflected, then
maybe in heaven there is no past or future. Or maybe
anything. At the moment, she still felt the physical
pain of her parents' death and was generally confused
about the universe. Her grandmother's direct criti-
cism of God had caused her to doubt numerous ideas
that she had previously taken for granted. These
things, coupled with the radical, physical changes she
was going through in this, her fourteenth year of life,
left her vastly perplexed.

For a long while Lisette remained in bed, watching

the light dance at the window, struggling to resolve her grand confusion. Eventually she was overwhelmed by the wobbly shape of her own extrapolations.

"Aghh," she groaned. "This is ridiculous." She threw back her covers, leapt from bed, stepped into her slippers, and crossed to the east window. When she drew back the drapes, a swell of sunlight surged into the room and bathed her in a pool of yellow warmth. (It takes a little over eight minutes for a wave of sunlight to travel the nearly ninety-three million miles from the sun to earth.) It was a healing warmth, naturally rich in optimism, and soon the iron vest that had been gripping her chest all week began to crumble and fall away. Suddenly she was able to breathe freely again. Suddenly she felt the promise of hope. She reached forward and hoisted the window sash, then stuck her head out and hollered, "Good-bye, Mom. Good-bye, Dad. I miss you, but I've got to quit this crazy crying. It's time to get on with my life."

Meanwhile, three stories below, Preston Sutter was blinking awake at the same rays of light that were resuscitating Lisette. Yet on him the sun had a contrary effect. Instead of optimism, he felt a wave of aggravation. He could not remember falling asleep, but the evidence was conclusive. Here he was, stiff and cranky, awaking in a rocking chair. Then he formulated his first thought of the day: Damn that boy.

Preston was sixty-six. Rising from his chair, he was reminded that life, after a certain point, is an accumulation of aches and pains. He had long ago inured himself to physical pain, yet the ache of losing Alison and Russel was a psychic hurt he could not easily ignore. These should have been his easy years—his soft reward for a life of honest toil—but *no*, that had been torn away. Now he was left to face his days mulling over what might have been.

His instincts told him Riley was safe, and he decided a few winks in his own bed would do no harm. Somehow, in the morning light, the matter of the boy's whereabouts seemed less pressing than the night before. If Riley had not returned when he awoke, well . . . he would deal with that problem then.

At about the same instant that Preston's head was hitting the proverbial pillow, Riley was being rudely awakened from a dream. He felt his leg jerk away from his hip, then he heard Thorpe's sharp command, "Let's go. It's already light out."

Riley sat up in the dark cave, wondering how Thorpe knew whether it was light or not. "Morning," he said. Instinctively he reached to touch his left forearm. A scab had formed during the night.

"Get moving," urged Thorpe. "If you aren't missing, then no one will come looking for you."

"I know," Riley mumbled as he felt around in the dark for his shoes. "We decided last night we'd get an early start."

"And I like doing what I decide."

"Give me a second."

"I've got your bag," Thorpe informed Riley as he dropped into the exit shaft.

"Antsy, aren't we," muttered Riley, but Thorpe was out of hearing range. Riley pulled on his shoes, crawled to the opening, and carefully inched his way into the shaft. At the bottom he squatted into a ball, then extended on his stomach. As he snaked through the narrow tunnel, it occurred to him that any creature much larger than he or Thorpe would not be able to follow.

When Riley emerged from the tunnel, he found Thorpe standing on a rock farther up the hill. Thorpe's hands were cupped behind his ears and his eyes swept methodically over the horizon.

Riley waited until his blood brother relaxed, apparently satisfied with his investigations, then groaned in a complaining manner. "I just remembered, I've got school tomorrow. I won't be able to come with any supplies until next Saturday."

"What's today?"

"Sunday."

Thorpe went blank for an instant (as though the thought of calendar days exhausted him), then he shrugged and jumped down on the ledge beside Riley. "Okay, we'll meet next Saturday. Make it noon, at Jagged Gap."

"Jagged Gap?!" blurted Riley. "Why, that's clear on the other end of the valley."

Thorpe rolled his eyes critically.

"Sorry." Riley blushed. "Which side of the river?"

"Just be there. I'll find you."

"And if you don't? Like maybe I can't make it, then what should I do to get in touch?"

Thorpe shook his head and sighed patiently. "You haven't even been awake for ten minutes and already you've started asking questions again."

"Sorry," said Riley. "Wait for me, though, if I'm late. I might have a problem getting away. Now, let's see—you said you wanted peanut butter, matches, tobacco, and flashlight batteries. Anything else?"

"Mostly I want peanut butter," Thorpe noted as he ducked into the thicket. "Now, come on. Pretend you're an Indian."

"Geronimo!" Riley called and plunged into the thicket.

Thorpe whipped around and grabbed Riley roughly by the front of his shirt. It was obvious from the look on his face that he was furious. "Don't you ever make loud noises when we're together. If you are traveling with me, it's your job to be invisible."

"Sorry."

"And quit saying sorry all the time."

After pancakes for breakfast, Clara and Lisette went to the garden and sat together on the chestnut bench. At their feet, a band of spring hyacinths, Spanish bluebells, and striped squills marched fragrantly around the reflecting pool. Usually on a Sunday morning, Lisette was with her mother in their regular pew at the Sparkling River Valley Methodist Church. The other Sutters rarely attended. Alison and Lisette did not go because they were hungry for religious instruction, they went because they were drawn to the church for the singing of hymns. For them it was simply a matter of pure fun to stand and blend their voices with the choir. Of the things Lisette knew she was going to miss the most, this weekly ritual of song was at the top of her list.

As for Clara, her usual activity on a sunny spring morning would involve snips or a trowel, and her thoughts would be of bulbs and seedlings. Yet today Clara was not thinking of plants; today she was dwelling on her newly inherited responsibility to oversee Lisette's upbringing as a woman. Lisette was already beginning to show physical signs of maturity, and Clara knew her granddaughter was entering a potentially tricky phase of life. As she saw it, it was now incumbent upon her to teach Lisette the secrets of being a lady. The girl must know the game; she must have the intelligent advantages of style. (As for Riley, Clara reflected, she and Preston would have to work on basic discipline before they could even consider imbuing him with the appropriate social skills.) Yet before anything could or should be done toward influencing Lisette's outward manners, Clara was sharply conscious of a need for inner healing. She did not want Lisette to forget the noble character of her parents, yet she also did not want her to bear the trauma of that loss through the rest of her life. It was imperative that her wounds not fester and leave a permanent scar. "Sweetheart," Clara began in a cheerful tone. "The world looks dark right now, but it will be bright again. I promise you that."

"I know, Grandma."

"Your mother and father were two of the happiest people to ever set foot on this earth. They wouldn't want you to be sad."

"I know."

"Did you know that their love for each other was the envy of everyone who knew them?"

"Maybe," Lisette allowed in a mouselike tone.

"It was like a golden fire when they were together,

with a flame that was never dampened by doubts. You must remember, they never, ever had any doubts about each other."

Lisette recalled an image of her mother and father by the river. Alison was in Russel's arms, and when she espied Lisette behind a tree, she flashed a bright smile over his shoulder and winked. Lisette shuddered with the memory. "Grandma, do you believe they are with the angels in heaven?"

Clara pursed her lips thoughtfully. "I'll be honest with you, dear; heaven and angels are not my speciality. I know that I believe in this world, in these flowers, in you, and in the things I see, but of heaven . . . I'm not sure."

"You aren't sure?" Lisette's disappointment was clear.

"Just because I'm not sure, it doesn't mean it isn't so," Clara replied softly. "Your mother and father believed . . . and so, perhaps they are in heaven."

"Then you think heaven does exist?"

"It does if you believe it does. I believe that believing is what stuck heaven up there to begin with."

"And what about the world?" Lisette asked with a touch of cynicism in her voice. "Does believing keep it here?"

Clara was not baited. "You must answer that for yourself."

Lisette looked around at the flowering world inside the stone walls. She saw pink azaleas, blue irises, orange lilies, red roses, mauve columbines, and yellow tulips. Beyond the walls were the lime-green boughs of budding fruit trees. Above, clean white clouds drifted under a pale blue sky. Yes, I believe in this. And I believe in heaven, too. "Grandma, this morning when I woke up I decided to be happy again . . . before I forget how."

"So wise," Clara whispered, wondering where some people got their strength. She knew that now was the time to give Lisette the legacy of her parents' love. From her breast pocket she withdrew a small gold locket and chain. The speech she had been preparing for this moment fled her mind and she said simply, "Lisette, I think you should have this."

Lisette accepted the familiar necklace without a word. Rare had been the occasion when her mother was not wearing the locket, although for some unknown reason, she had not donned it on that day she died. After holding the necklace for a reverent moment, Lisette pressed open the clasp and read: *Such is our love that even the angels in heaven are impressed.*

Clara's voice cracked on the edge of a cry. "Your father gave that to your mother before they were married."

• • •

Thorpe and Riley stopped in the woods near the foot of the Upper Place driveway. Thorpe handed him his tent and blanket. Then, for the umpteenth time, he warned, "Just remember, Riley, you swore you never saw me."

Riley pointed to the fresh scab on his left forearm. "How could I forget?"

Thorpe extended his left arm. His cut had been slow in healing. It was surrounded by blotches of crusted blood. "I hate to keep saying it—of course I trust my own blood brother. It's just that sometimes people slip up and say things. You have to pretend you never even heard my name."

"Don't worry about me," Riley said, then saluted.

Thorpe nodded appreciatively.

"Thanks again for getting me out of that tree."

A rare smile flitted across Thorpe's face. "Anyone that can fly off Bluff Top with a tent deserves to be rescued."

Riley sensed the opportunity to repeat a question that had gone unanswered the night before. "So, why'd you run away? You said you'd tell me."

All remnants of humor left Thorpe's face. "I said I might think about telling you."

Riley accepted the rebuff without argument. "Okay. Sorry. Tell me some other time if you want. See you Saturday."

"Right," Thorpe mumbled, then turned to lope away.

As Riley watched Thorpe disappear into the woods, a part of him longed to chuck it all and follow his new friend. Then a more responsible aspect of his character groaned and turned him toward the big brick home on the hill. In the previous twenty hours he had given little thought to how his grandparents might react to his absence, and so now he began to worry double-time.

He stole quickly across the front lawn and circled the house toward the back porch. As he passed the arbored entrance to the garden, he glanced in and saw Lisette and Clara. Lisette sensed his presence and turned. Clara, alerted by her movement, also turned. Riley froze. Written in bold letters across his forehead was the word *guilty*.

Clara jumped from the bench and set her hands on her hips. She was clearly in no mood for pleasantries. "What have you got to say for yourself?"

"I got lost," Riley mumbled.

"Lost?" Clara took a step in his direction. "You took a tent with you, and you got lost?"

"Yes, ma'am. Sort of."

"You did not get lost," Clara barked. "What you did was worry your grandfather."

Riley took a sudden interest in his shoes. "Sorry."

"Sorry?!" Clara shouted. "I suppose that makes everything okay."

Riley continued to study his shoes.

"You get this straight right now, young man. As long as you are living here, you are to obey your grandfather and me, *always*. And you are to go out of your way to avoid giving your Pa-Preston even the smallest cause for worry."

"Yes, ma'am."

" 'Yes, ma'am' what?"

"I won't worry Pa-Preston."

Clara pointed. "Go in the house and tell him that."

Riley turned and began to shuffle away.

In a softer, somewhat forgiving tone, Clara added, "He's in his bedroom. Be careful when you wake him."

Four

Nineteen sixty-nine was a red-letter year in North America, a time rife with technological advances and cultural change. Two humans walked on the moon. It was the heyday of the love crowd: power to the people. Public protests against government policies were passionate and frequent, see-through fashions appeared on certain city streets, and mind-expanding drugs were available for three dollars a tablet at most institutions of higher learning.

The zeitgeist was wearing flowers in her hair. For many a new way of life was dawning.

Partially because of its geographic isolation, and partially because of the inherently nostalgic mind-set of mountain people in general, Bluff County remained a long way from the cutting edge of change in 1969. Technology had yet to solve the problem of poor television reception in the valleys, and the notion of cultural transformation meant marrying someone who was not your cousin. There were no see-through garments (unless a blouse got wet by accident), and minds were bent—not expanded—with old-fashioned moonshine. Public protest was limited to the actions of a handful of radical seniors from the local high school who expressed their angst by painting STUFF THE BLUFF on roadside barns, bridge trestles, and water towers.

In small communities, what happens to one happens to all.

The sudden demise of Alison and Russel Sutter spread over Bluff County like a deprivation bomb. The Sutter family had been a symbol of stability in that area of the mountains for too many generations to remember, and the swift, arbitrary finality of the accident reminded the local people of their own fragile vulnerability. Some of the good residents of those ancient hills already understood that they would feel the lack of this golden couple long after the shock of the loss had diminished.

Grace is given and grace is taken away.

On Monday morning when Lisette and Riley returned to their respective schools—Lisette to the high school, where she was in the ninth grade, and Riley to Little Bluff Elementary, where he was in the seventh—they found themselves to be the recipients of sympathy from the faculty, and the objects of morbid curiosity to their schoolmates. Both schools were on the small side, with approximately fifty students per grade, and it was virtually impossible for either sibling to blend into the background.

"Still waters run deep," was what the teachers said about Lisette. (In this year of her physical transformation, no one except Riley remembered to call her Mousey.) She returned to her classes as more or less the same shy, studious girl she had always been. Perhaps she was quieter than before, but generally she seemed to have accepted the turn in her life and begun to adapt. Every day she wore the locket, and that gave her strength.

It was Riley who had changed the most. Once a gregarious cutup, he now detached himself behind a stoic mask and showed a cool disregard for the diversionary antics of his classmates. His old gang felt a sharp lack of leadership, and were disappointed that Riley had abandoned them to their own pranks. Still, their respect for him did not dwindle. Instead, it increased. The aloof glimmer they now saw in his eyes suggested to them that Riley was dwelling in a private world that they might never enter.

Riley's teachers were delighted with his new, reserved demeanor, although they regretted that his lackadaisical study habits had not improved with his exterior transformation. He was polite but unteachable . . . lost in his own reflections. His only apparent interests were the clock on the wall and the bell that tolled at the end of each day.

Of course, neither Riley's teachers nor his classmates knew that he now had a blood brother who lived in a hidden cave and smoked a stolen pipe.

Riley did manage to rendezvous with Thorpe at Jagged Gap on the Saturday following their first meeting, but their time together was limited by Riley's need to return home before late afternoon. Basically, he had a few moments to deliver the peanut butter, flashlight batteries, and other items that he had obtained, and then start back for the Upper Place. The Sutters were invited for dinner at the Applegates', and try as he did, there was no way Riley could wrangle out of going.

Thorpe drew back on his slingshot and launched a rock at an isolated tree on the opposite bank of the river. It hit its mark with an accurate *thwack*. "Thanks for the supplies."

"No need to thank me." Riley shrugged. "I'm just sorry I have to go."

"You sure are sorry a lot," Thorpe remarked with a dry grin.

"I know. It's a habit with me," Riley readily admitted. "Still, I wish I didn't have to leave."

Thorpe fired another accurate shot across the river,

then offered in a friendly tone, "I had fun last week . . . actually talking to somebody. I'd almost forgotten that I like people."

"I had fun, too."

Thorpe stared thoughtfully at the river, then shrugged. "So, you better go."

"Yeah. Okay. Next week I'll try to get permission to camp out. Where do I find you?"

"Come to the hills near the cave. I'll be looking for you."

Riley started homeward. After walking a short distance along the riverbank, it occurred to him that Thorpe seemed kind of lonely. He turned to wave a final good-bye, but by then his blood brother had already disappeared.

As much as Riley resisted the whole idea of dressing up and minding his manners as a guest at someone else's dinner table, he had to admit that old Judge Applegate and his peppy, white-haired wife were pretty nice people. In fact, Riley got the impression that Phyllis Applegate liked kids as much as, if not more than, she liked adults. Not only did she make a point to include him and Lisette in the general conversation at the table, but she also asked interesting questions, and then would actually listen to the answers.

There was one other thing that Riley had to admit, which was that Lisette was growing up fast. In his mind, she appeared to have transformed overnight. With her erect posture, her neatly pressed blouse, her carefully braided hair, and her fine manners, it almost seemed as if there was a stranger at the table.

After dinner, during that soft hour of light before sunset, Riley and Lisette accompanied Phyllis Applegate on a walk to see the bubbling springs at the rear of the property. They left the house by way of a small courtyard, then followed a landscaped path for about a hundred yards. It ended at the foot of Bluff Top Ridge, where the five varied-sized springs gushed from beneath the mountain.

While Riley occupied himself by thoroughly examining each of the spring pools, Lisette sat with Phyllis in a gazebo built on a rock near the largest pool. Although the two were separated in age by more than fifty years, there was a sincere quality to Phyllis that bridged all gaps. And as Lisette was soon to find out, they shared an attraction to the mysterious side of life.

"Is that Alison's locket you're wearing?"

"Yes." Lisette fingered the chain at her neck and blushed.

"She was so beautiful," Phyllis sighed.

"Dad gave it to her."

"I know. Alison was very proud of that locket. I don't think I ever saw her without it on."

Lisette considered telling Phyllis that her mother had not been wearing the locket on the day of the accident, but then decided it was an irrelevant fact that need not be shared.

It seemed clear to Phyllis that Lisette was looking for some kind of meaning in the empty aftermath of her loss, and she felt compelled to help. "I'm sure the locket was sacred to Alison."

"Sacred?" Lisette repeated softly, eager to learn what she could about Alison or the locket. "Do you mean holy?"

A ray of sweetness illuminated Phyllis's angular face. "Holy as it relates to devotion in a singular belief. For your parents, I think, that belief was in each other, and the locket was a symbol of their devotion."

The word *belief* reminded Lisette of Clara's ambiguity on the question of heaven, and she sensed that this was a good time to seek a second opinion. "Do you think Mom and Dad are together?"

Phyllis did not hesitate. "Certainly they are together. They were never the type to let a little thing like death come between them."

Lisette was slightly taken aback by Phyllis's odd humor—if indeed it was humor—yet she was also impressed by the ring of veracity in her voice.

"Grandma wasn't so sure about heaven. She said it's just an idea held in place by belief."

"With all due respect to the impeccable character of Clara Sutter," Phyllis avowed solemnly, "I assure you there is a world beyond this one."

Lisette subconsciously reached to her chest and touched the locket while staring silently at the elder hostess.

Phyllis could see that Lisette wanted to ask how she knew there was another world. She smiled sweetly. "Let me tell you a little story."

"Please," Lisette said softly.

Phyllis collected her thoughts with a deep sigh. "When I was a young lady—not much older than you are now, and certainly not as pretty—I lived in Richmond. And quite frequently my family came to Bluff County to visit our cousins in Clear Glen. Perhaps you know the Jeeters."

"I've heard the name."

"I was Jeeter before I got married," said Phyllis. "Anyway, we were visiting one weekend in October—I believe I was sixteen at the time—and someone had organized a hayride for the night of the full moon. The Hunter's moon, they call it. There were a couple of children and a handful of adults on the wagon, but mostly it was teenagers that night. About twenty of us. I remember the sky was perfectly clear and the moon was nearly bright enough to read by. It was chilly. I can still hear the horses snorting and whinnying as they strained to carry us up the mountain. There were three in the team. All white."

Lisette moaned. "Ooh. It sounds so . . . exciting."

"It was," Phyllis agreed. "Especially for a city girl like me. And it was made even more exciting by the presence of one handsome young man on the wagon . . . someone whom I could not stop thinking about the whole night. But then, well, I was shy, and so was he, and although we kept stealing glances at each other, we never spoke. It was terribly disconcerting."

Although Lisette was unsure of exactly what disconcerting meant, she adjoined sympathetically, "I bet it was."

Phyllis smiled, then grew serious again. "So, the ride was almost over. We were coming down the mountain, and I was feeling sad because I had not spoken with the handsome boy. Then suddenly a car came speeding around a curve. The driver flashed the headlights and blew the horn, which startled the poor horses. They reared up, the wagon tipped sideways, and I was thrown into an embankment." Phyllis paused to make eye contact with her listener.

Lisette stared back with undivided attention.

"I must have been knocked unconscious. I'm not sure, but the next thing I knew I was floating up-

wards in a kind of bright and silent funnel of air. Way
below I could see the mountains and the road, and a
crowd of people scrambling around the overturned
wagon. I remember this wonderful, free feeling . . .
like everything was made of goodness. Then I
thought, I'm rising up to heaven. I don't know how
I knew that, but it was clear to me."

Phyllis exchanged looks with Lisette, who sat
slack-jawed in suspense.

"So there I was," Phyllis continued in a soft, con-
fiding voice, "floating upwards into heaven, when
suddenly I could feel a presence beside me. I could
not see it, but I knew it was there. And then I heard
a voice."

"A voice?!" Lisette blurted. For the moment she
had forgotten her troubles. Mrs. Applegate's provoca-
tive tale had transported her to another place and
time.

"Yes, a voice," Phyllis repeated. "I'm not sure
where it came from, but I heard it as clear as a bell
in my head. It said: 'This is not your time. Go back.
Someone is waiting for you.' "

"Oh, wow. Unbelievable."

"Yet it happened," said Phyllis.

"Oh, I didn't mean it wasn't true," Lisette stammered.

As much to herself as to Lisette, Phyllis smiled before resuming her story. "After I heard the voice, the next thing I knew I was on the ground, and I could feel someone touching my neck to check for a pulse. When I opened my eyes, there was the handsome boy leaning over me."

"Amazing," Lisette whispered.

"It was amazing." Phyllis nodded. "And that is why I am able to assure you there is a world beyond this one."

"Wow. Whatever happened to the boy?"

"He became a man." Phyllis grinned. "Then we got married."

"Oh," gushed Lisette. "It was the judge."

Phyllis sighed, turned a sweeping gaze over Bluff Top, then said softly, "Lisette, may I tell you what I suspect?"

"Yes. Please do."

"Well, I suspect that as long as you are wearing the locket, your parents will watch over you."

"They will?"

Phyllis nodded affirmatively. "Either they will watch or they will ask an angel to do the job."

"An angel? Like a cherub with wings?" Lisette was not quite sure if Phyllis was speaking literally or metaphorically.

There was no mockery in her voice when she laughed. "Cherubs are too mischievous for that kind of work. You would have a guardian angel. And because they do much of their work here on earth, they usually don't have wings."

After an uncertain pause, Lisette confessed, "Do you mean . . . are there really such things as guardian angels?"

Phyllis's kind smile suggested that she was amused rather than bothered by Lisette's doubtful tone. "Oh, yes indeed, guardian angels exist. Of course, they are mostly spirit, and because of that, they exist in subtle ways. But sometimes—and this is hard to explain— the spirit will associate very closely with a person, and in a gentle way they will persuade, or rather guide, that person to act. And thus . . . in a sense, that person becomes a guardian angel. In those cases, they are very real."

Twilight was falling as they started back for the house. Riley raced ahead of Lisette and Phyllis, only slowing his pace as he reached the door to the courtyard. He heard something there that halted him in his tracks. It was the judge's deliberate voice. It had just said the name Greenwood. The next sentence was muffled, but Riley thought he could discern the words: Ten, with five years suspended for mitigating circumstances. She could be out in three.

Riley wanted to burst into the courtyard and ask,

"Who?" but some mixture of memory and instinct told him they were speaking of Thorpe's mother. Vaguely, he remembered there had been a big scandal around the time of Thorpe's disappearance. He wished now that he had paid more attention to the talk.

Riley heard Clara say something about "the boy," to which Judge Applegate replied, "No. Not yet." Then, much to Riley's chagrin, Lisette and Phyllis appeared at his back and he was no longer able to eavesdrop.

The subject was promptly dropped as the trio entered the courtyard. Filled though he was with curiosity, Riley recalled his blood brother's command to never mention his name in public, so he suppressed the urge to ask any of the questions that were burning on the tip of his tongue.

Preston drove the long way home, heading south along the west side of Bluff Top Ridge toward the range of low hills at Jagged Gap. Riley sat with his head partially out of the rear window, letting the wind make sounds in his open mouth and blow his sandy hair backward. As he watched the brown-green blur of the woods passing on his left, his thoughts went out to his fugitive blood brother. With his thoughts went his heart. Where are you now? Why have they put your mother in prison?

Gazing from the opposite side of Preston's Buick, Lisette also watched the brown-green blur of the passing woods. She fingered the necklace at her neck and wondered if her parents had found her a guardian angel. Then she heard Phyllis Applegate's name and her thoughts took an abrupt turn toward the front seat.

"She is such a sweet dear," allowed Clara.

"Yes," agreed Preston. "And of all the people in the world, it seems a particular shame with her."

"Life is funny that way," mused Clara.

Lisette could not restrain her curiosity. "What? What about Mrs. Applegate?"

"Oh." Clara sighed as if it was nothing. "All her life she and the judge have wanted a family; she's crazy about children, but as luck would have it, they've never had any of their own."

"I think she feels she's let down the judge," Preston said with a note of tenderness.

Clara pursed her lips at some private thought, then suddenly began to chuckle. "Knowing Phyllis, she's still optimistic about her chances."

Five

Although May of 1969 was a green and glorious month in the Blue Ridge Mountains, to Riley, it seemed to drag on like an eternity. Since late in April when he had parachuted into the secret world of Thorpe Greenwood, he had only managed three quick trips into the mountains to meet with his blood brother. They were supply runs, really; good for keeping in touch, but not much in the way of developing their friendship or actually having any fun. Riley was frustrated. At school he grew increasingly more aloof from his mates, and at home he spent many solitary hours sitting on the roof of the Upper Place, gazing westward toward Bluff Top Ridge.

Eventually June sixth arrived and school let out for summer vacation. Riley wasted no time in clearing his schedule. At supper on the evening of the sixth he informed his grandparents that he would not be signing up for Little League. "It's too far to drive just to play baseball," he reasoned. "I'd rather just hang around here and do some camping in the mountains."

"But Riley," Clara protested. "I thought you were the star shortstop. Won't your team be disappointed?"

"Nah." Riley shrugged. "Besides, it's just a game."

Preston approved. He had grown up in the surrounding hills and knew the thrill of exploring them as a boy. "Fine, if that's what you prefer," he informed his independent grandson. "But we won't tolerate you going off without permission—not like last time. The rule is this: You only go when Clara or I say you go, and we agree beforehand on when you return."

"Thank you, Pa-Preston." Riley could hardly contain his excitement. "May I go tomorrow for two nights?"

Preston ignored the request. "Break that rule, and you'll lose the privilege altogether."

"I won't break any rules," Riley said assuringly. "So, how about tomorrow? Two nights. Please?"

"Aren't you afraid of bears?" Clara teased.

"No."

"I guess you're not afraid of rattlesnakes, either."

"Rattlers don't live around here," Riley scoffed at Clara, then turned to his grandfather for confirmation. "Do they?"

"Not many." Preston shook his head. "On occasion you might find one sunning on a ledge, or near a cave where they like to nest, but generally rattlers are pretty scarce this far east."

Caves, ledges . . . Riley made a mental note to ask Thorpe if he had ever encountered a rattler, then resumed pressing his case. "So, can I go tomorrow, or what?"

"Good Lord, boy," Preston snickered. "Yes, you can go, but I think one night is enough for this first trip."

"Okay," said Riley. He knew one night was better than none.

Clara was concerned about Lisette being isolated at the Upper Place during the summer months. She was of the school of thought that said young women of a certain age need other young women of a similar age with whom to discuss their problems. And so she got on the phone and called Melinda Kidder. Melinda was a single, working mother who had been a close friend of Alison and Russel. Her daughter, Kissy, was thirteen.

"That's entirely copacetic with me, Mrs. Sutter," Melinda chimed when Clara proposed that Kissy spend much of the summer at the Upper Place. "I think it would do both girls good, and it'd be a blessing for me not to worry about what she was up to every day."

Kissy Kidder was one of those giggling, grinning packages of warmth that give humankind such a good name. She was tall and gangly, and had a head full of frizzy, carrot-colored hair. Her eyes were green, and her white teeth flashed when she laughed, which was often and loudly.

When Clara informed her granddaughter that Kissy would be visiting them for most of the summer, the mere thought of her presence caused Lisette to break out in paroxysms of glee.

Riley's two days and one night in the mountains with Thorpe did not go exactly as he had envisioned. On the afternoon when he arrived at the hidden cave— his bags heavy with supplies and his spirits bolstered with the promise of real adventure—Thorpe was not there to greet him. After waiting in the dark chamber for more than an hour (the crickets were driving him nuts, so he took the liberty of burning one of Thorpe's precious candles), he crawled out and waited an additional several hours on the ledge near the entrance hole. As the sun followed its slow arc over the ridge, his mood alternated between disappointment and anger.

It was nearly dusk when he felt a tap on his shoulder and heard Thorpe's terse voice. "Man, you got a lot to learn."

"What?" Riley replied defensively, turning and widening his eyes at the sight of blood on Thorpe's hands.

"You're sitting out in the open, right by the entrance to my home. Do you want to give me away?"

"No, of course not. There's nobody around here."

"How do you know?" Thorpe asked sharply. "I got close enough to touch you before you even knew I was here."

Riley got the point. "Sorry. I won't do it again."

Thorpe glared critically at Riley and shook his head. "I can see you're going to need some training."

Riley blushed, and then hoping to divert Thorpe's wrathful stare, he asked, "Where've you been? What happened to your hands?"

Thorpe reached into a cloth sack hanging from his shoulder and withdrew a freshly gutted rabbit. The sight of the dead creature made Riley wince. "I've been doing what I do every day," said Thorpe.

"What's that?" Riley asked without thinking.

"Surviving." Thorpe smiled. "It's all the latest rage."

Immediately upon entering the cave, Thorpe went about the business of building a small fire. Afterward he sharpened his knife on a whetstone, expertly skinned the rabbit, put it on a spit, then sat back and smoked while he waited for the hare to cook. Riley tried several times to spark up a conversation, yet each attempt at dialogue was quickly rebuffed by a thorny look from Thorpe. He did not know whether his blood brother was still mad at him for sitting out near the cave entrance, or if he was just in a sour mood. Whatever, it was apparent he had a lot on his mind and wished for silence.

Later, after a meal of stringy rabbit meat, Thorpe offered something of an explanation for his stony behavior. "You know, Riley, when you're on your own the way I am, survival is not a game. In fact, it's a very serious business. I have my reasons for being out here. They are what they are, and there's not much room for sentimental stuff." Thorpe let his words hang for a moment in the smoke-filled den.

Riley wanted to ask what the reasons were, but he knew now was not the time to speak. He held his tongue and waited.

Soon, in a more appeasing tone, Thorpe resumed. "Before I helped you out of the tree that day, I'd gone ten months without having a conversation. And it didn't bother me one bit. I liked it. But since we met and became blood brothers, I know there's the chance you might come and I'll have someone to talk with. Just knowing that, well . . . it makes it harder to be alone. Now I know what I'm missing, and it reminds me that I don't have a normal life."

"Sorry," said Riley.

Riley looked so hangdog and guilty that Thorpe could not help but laugh. "Hey, I don't blame you. I thought about it, and I've decided that loneliness isn't so bad."

Riley blushed with a kind of sympathetic embarrassment. He wished he could think of the right thing to say.

"I mean . . . well, I can deal with it all right. The main thing for me is to survive."

"Yeah, you gotta survive."

"Right," Thorpe agreed with a thin smile. "And tomorrow I'm going to teach you a few tricks of the trade."

From early the next morning when they crawled into the open world, until midday when Riley returned to the Upper Place, Thorpe instructed him in the fundamentals of life on the lam. There were certain technical points, such as reading the wind and understanding the way sound travels around obstacles, but most of what Thorpe taught him was mental. "It's an attitude. You must learn to think invisible."

"Think invisible?"

"Make believe like you don't exist."

"Sorry if I seem stupid, but how do I do that?"

Patiently, and with complete earnestness, Thorpe explained. "I find it helps if you pretend like someone is hunting you, and if you let them catch you, you'll be skinned alive. It kind of gives you a certain feeling."

"Oh, yeah," mused Riley. "Now I get it."

And so began the summer of 1969 in the valleys and mountains of Bluff County. Slowly, day by day, week by week, the Sutters and everyone else in their world were carried another step away from that mean convulsion in time when Alison and Russel plummeted into a gulley and were consumed by fire. Slowly, hearts began to heal and faith was restored to the faithful. Even at the Upper Place, a benign sort of forgetfulness began to take hold.

Most days Riley was either off in the hills with Thorpe or at home plotting for permission to return there. Lisette and Kissy more or less lived on the front porch, where they played imaginary games, talked and giggled about people they knew, and filled the air around them with much-needed mirth. Sometimes when Riley was around he joined them in their conversations, but generally he kept to himself. Clara busied herself anticipating everyone's domestic needs, and when those chores were done, she slipped into her garden to prune, preen, and pamper her flowers. Preston was never sure what to do. Basically he puttered about, maintaining the lawns or fixing something in the house, always taking time for a nap between activities.

Meanwhile, across the wooded canyon and over the ridge, old Judge Applegate and his gentle, gracious wife, Phyllis, continued to live in peaceable retirement. Occasionally she called Clara or Clara called her, but well over a month would pass before she and Lisette would get together for another one of their mystical talks.

One pleasant, if not too hot, day in mid-June, Kissy and Lisette concluded that they were bored on the porch. They decided they should go somewhere.

"But where?"

"Anywhere. I don't care."

"Fine. I'll follow you."

"No, it was your idea. You lead the way."

"I'll lead if you pick the direction."

"Easy." Kissy giggled. She closed her eyes, spun around, and pointed in the general direction of Richmond. "That way."

They walked around the walled garden, entered the overgrown field on the south slope of the plateau, climbed over a crumbling stone wall, passed through a stand of loblolly pine, then stepped into the shade of the hardwood forest. Here the sky was all but obscured by towering oak, elm, hickory, and maple trees. It was a vast forest that extended southeast from the plateau, spread across the head of the valley, and reached all the way to the banks of the Sparkling River.

There was little vegetation growing on the shaded forest floor and the girls found the going relatively easy. Perhaps the going was too easy. A mixture of enchantment and adolescent enthusiasm for discovery drew them further and deeper into the unfamiliar woods.

After walking merrily along for twenty minutes, it suddenly occurred to them that they were lost.

"Which way now?"

"I'm following you." There was no humor in Kissy's voice.

Lisette looked around. She saw only an endless arrangement of tree trunks and giant, upward-thrusting limbs. It would have been easier for her to choose a direction if she had known where they were trying to go, but since they had begun their journey without a chosen destination, she was severely handicapped.

Lisette sensed that Kissy was about to panic. Being older and generally responsible to begin with, she felt it was her duty to conceal her own doubts and convey calm. She clutched at the necklace around her neck, whispered a silent prayer for help, then pretended to peer about for a specific landmark.

It all looked the same, yet soon Lisette had a hunch. She released the locket and pointed to an obscure break in the trees. "Let's take that path."

"What path?"

"That one. Come on," Lisette commanded confidently. She took Kissy by the arm and tugged.

Serendipity is the luck of finding something special you did not know you were searching for in the first place. It is just the stuff you want when you are in a large forest looking for anywhere—or rather, nowhere in particular. The girls followed Lisette's invisible path for approximately a hundred yards when serendipity struck. The woods suddenly parted and they found themselves standing on a moss-covered knoll overlooking a sunlit meadow. The meadow was replete with wildflowers, a winding stream, songbirds, butterflies, bobtails, ferns, and tall grasses.

Lisette felt a chill of astonishment. It was a scene out of an ancient fable. Instinctively she touched the locket at her chest. Then she recalled Phyllis Applegate's words about an angel being assigned to watch over her. The meadow was almost too perfect. It made her wonder if perhaps, just maybe, she had been guided to this spot.

Kissy giggled at their good fortune. "Looks like we found the anywhere we were looking for."

"Yes it does," Lisette concurred with a growing grin.

They plopped down on the green carpet and removed their shoes. (Neither girl noticed the fat toad they had disturbed. It frowned and hopped angrily away.)

"It's so beautiful here!" exclaimed Kissy.

"Absolutely gorgeous. Like a dream."

"Like a sweet dream. So . . . what do you want to do now?"

Lisette paused to consider, then smiled broadly. "Momma used to say that singing was praying twice."

"Ooh. I love it when you sing," Kissy gushed.

"It's been a while," noted Lisette. And then, without further ado, she lifted her soprano voice and sang:

> *"From this valley they say you are going,*
> *We will miss your bright eyes and sweet smile.*
> *For they say you are taking the sunshine*
> *That brightens our pathway awhile."*

Kissy, an alto, sang harmony on the chorus.

> *"Come and sit by my side if you love me*
> *Do not hasten to bid me adieu*

> *But remember the Red River Valley*
> *And the girl who loves you so true."*

Earlier in the day when the girls left the house, Riley had been watching from the kitchen window. He had returned from the mountains the evening before and was now bound to the immediate vicinity of the Upper Place. Consequently he did not know what to do with himself—not until he saw Lisette and Kissy heading into the woods. To him, it seemed only logical that they should be tailed.

He had followed them at a distance, employing all the techniques of concealment and stealth that Thorpe had been teaching him.

And so now, as Lisette continued with the third verse of "The Red River Valley," Riley stood listening from behind a tree on the west side of the meadow.

> *"Won't you think of the valley you're leaving?*
> *Oh, how lonely, how sad it will be.*
> *Oh, think of the fond heart you're breaking*
> *And the grief you are causing me to see."*

Riley knew singing was a passion that Lisette had shared with their mother, and as he listened to her voice rising into the sky, he felt suddenly proud of his sister. He also felt a pang of guilt for having virtually ignored Lisette since the week of the funeral, when he formed his blood pact with Thorpe. Now, moved by her fine voice, he felt an urge to make amends.

Life is nothing if it is not full of surprises: Just as Riley was about to step into the open and reveal his presence by applauding, he was frozen by a nearby sound. "Pssst."

He spun around, seeing no one.

"Pssst."

He craned his neck and looked up just as a blur dropped from a nearby tree. It was Thorpe. He raised an index finger to his lips in a signal for silence, then motioned for Riley to follow.

As the blood brothers ran west from the meadow, they were serenaded by a repeat refrain of "The Red River Valley."

Soon Thorpe halted in a clearing and sat down. "Man," he sighed. "Those girls sure can sing."

"Yes. They're pretty good," Riley agreed as he fell to the ground. "So, what are you doing here?"

"Same as you—observing. I was in the field by the garden when your sister and her friend walked right past me. I saw you coming, too."

"How do you know that's my sister?"

"It's obvious. You both have the same little noses. Who is the carrot-top?"

"Kissy. Lisette's friend from Clear Glen," replied

Riley, before inquiring in a suspicious tone, "Thorpe, were you casing our house?"

"Nah. Of course not." Thorpe shrugged innocently. "I was just getting a look at where you live."

"You were casing us, weren't you?"

Thorpe appeared hurt by the accusation. "Do you really think I'd steal from my own blood brother? That's preposterous."

After considering for a second, Riley realized his mistake. "Sorry. It's just that you told me you like to observe a place before you venture in after supplies."

Thorpe ignored the comment. He leaned back on his elbows and peered into the overhead foliage. The dreamy, far-off expression that settled over his face was a look that Riley had never seen before. It seemed almost as if Thorpe were drunk. "So," he said, sighing. "Your sister's name is Lisette?"

"Yep. She's fourteen."

"You never told me she was interesting."

"Interesting?" Riley was baffled. "You never asked."

Thorpe released his elbows and dropped on his back. "She has curves."

"Excuse me?"

"Curves. Like a woman."

"Yeah, right." Riley nodded, then added as an afterthought, "All that happened this year."

"Listen."

Floating lightly through the forest came the dulcet sound of two clear, adolescent voices:

> *"Come and sit by my side if you love me*
> *Do not hasten to bid me adieu*
> *But remember the Red River Valley*
> *And the girl that has loved you so true."*

Thorpe moaned happily. Then, with a far, far, far-away look in his eyes, he mused, "That song . . . it gets me every time."

Six

—

During the next week as Riley waited out the requisite days before he was permitted to return to the mountains, he thought often about the curious, haunted look he had seen on Thorpe's face while the girls were singing. It was a look of intensely private, inner reflection, and it reminded Riley that there was much about Thorpe's character that he did not understand. Although he was unremittingly cautious and always sharply aware of his surroundings, he was subject to a variety of changeable moods. Sometimes he was stern and serious, other times he was high-spirited and humorous, and on many occasions he was distracted and tense. Riley had learned to expect the unexpected when visiting Thorpe.

Later that week when he was finally free to return to the mountains and rendezvous with Thorpe, Riley was well served in expecting the unexpected. Otherwise he would have been more shocked than he was by the botched haircut his blood brother had suffered upon himself. At a glance it appeared as if Thorpe had taken a buck knife to his head in anger. (Although neither boy realized it at the time, Thorpe Greenwood had anticipated the punk movement by more than a decade.)

"So . . ." Thorpe fidgeted with his slingshot. "What do you think?"

Riley reacted with a tactful silence. Thorpe's hands, face, and what remained of his hair had been thoroughly washed. Not only that, but his clothes were almost clean and he no longer emanated the dank odor of a troglodyte.

"So, how do I look?" Thorpe pressed for feedback. It was apparent he valued Riley's opinion.

"It'll take some getting used to."

"What do you mean, 'getting used to'?"

"Hmm . . . I'd say . . ." Riley stalled while he searched for the right thing to say. "Well, I'd say you look pretty decent."

"You think so?"

"Sure. Compared to some kids, you look great."

"Thanks." Thorpe grinned proudly. "The way I figure it, just because I live like an old hermit, it doesn't mean I have to let my grooming get out of control."

"Of course not," agreed Riley. Then, only too eager to change the subject, he reached into his pack and withdrew a paper bag. "I've got oatmeal-raisin cookies."

"Great. My favorite."

"I only brought five. They're my Pa-Preston's favorite, too."

"The greedy old fart," chortled Thorpe.

That afternoon Thorpe informed Riley that it was time to check the lodge at the Stills Bend Hunt Club. He wanted to see if they had restocked their cupboards. As he explained, the lodge was a regular source of basic provisions, such as salt, sugar, and tobacco. "I only go once every five or six weeks, and then I just take a few things. Don't want to arouse any suspicions."

"That's smart."

"I'm not so sure it's smart to keep going back there or not," Thorpe said in a reserved tone. "But it is necessary."

Riley felt honored to accompany Thorpe on an actual raid. To Riley it signified a new level of acceptance. We blood brothers like to stick together, he thought smugly to himself.

The boys hiked south along the top of the ridge until they reached its conclusion, then descended into the woods at the north end of Broken Valley. From there it was just a quick jaunt across Fast Creek to an old red-clay fire lane that led up to the lodge on the hill. When they reached the lane, Thorpe knelt to investigate for recent tracks. After detecting nothing fishy, he announced that the coast was clear.

The lodge was a large, simply designed log structure built in a small clearing on top of a knoll. It had a cedar shake roof and a thick fieldstone chimney. Weeds grew up by the foundation and reached to the bottom of shuttered windows. Crude plank-board steps climbed to a solid-looking oak door. It was secured by a slide bolt and an iron lock. Tacked in plain view on the door was a sign that read:

STILLS BEND HUNT CLUB, MEMBERS ONLY.

TRESPASSERS WILL EITHER BE SHOT OR PROSECUTED

TO THE FULLEST EXTENT OF THE LAW.

"So that's it, huh?" Riley whispered as he and Thorpe hid in the bushes on the far side of the clearing.

"Yep. It's where I do most of my shopping."

"The place looks kind of spooky to me."

"Yeah, it is spooky, but the prices are right."

Doing his best to convey nonchalance, Riley asked, "So, how do you get in there?"

"In the back of the lodge, up top, there's a window loose. You have to shimmy up a pole to get to it.

Then it's easy. The window pulls away at the wall and there's enough room to squeeze through. After that you drop down on a bunk bed and you're in. Piece of cake."

Riley strained to hide his growing nervousness. He had never broken into a building before.

"You coming?"

"Me? Oh . . . I figured you'd want me to be your lookout."

"I've never had a lookout before," Thorpe noted.

Riley was slightly embarrassed, yet firm in his decision. "I'm sorry, but I'd rather wait here."

Thorpe understood Riley's concern. "No need to be sorry. It's fine with me if you wait. After all, there's no use making outlaws out of both of us. I'll be back in a jiffy."

Thorpe had been gone for all of one minute when Riley heard the sound of an engine revving in the near distance. As he cocked his ears to zero in on the sound, his spirits sank sharply. It was a truck, or a jeep, and it was coming up the hill.

Riley darted into the clearing and whistled. There was no response. He whistled again, and again there was no response. What to do? Thorpe was probably already inside.

Riley considered running to the lodge and hollering, but before he could make a decision, the revving engine was almost upon him. He dove back into the bushes just a second before a pickup truck lurched over the rise and entered the clearing. It halted near the front steps of the lodge. The engine was shut off, then two men stepped out and looked idly around. Riley slid deeper into the bushes, remembering to invoke his invisible self as Thorpe had taught him. The men moved to the back of the truck, where they each grabbed a box of supplies. Then they started for the porch. One of them had a set of keys in his hand.

Thorpe was in the kitchen when he heard the truck. For an instant he froze, his heart racing with fear. There was no time to put things back in order. He quickly stuffed a few supplies in his bag and started toward the bunk bed.

The sound of booted footsteps on the porch fell like the cold hand of the reaper on his shoulders. He was not going to make it. As he swung himself up on the top bunk, he heard the sound of a key turning in the lock.

In his haste to get out, he caused the window to jam in its frame. The clank of a slide bolt echoed through his mind like a death knell. This is it, he thought, they've got me.

Then he heard his lookout's voice.

"Hey! Help!" Riley called in a frightened manner.

The men turned and gazed across the clearing.

"Gosh, I'm glad to see you guys. I've been lost for hours. How do I get out of here?" Riley bit his lower lip and feigned helplessness. Then, for added effect, he pretended to fight back tears.

The two men exchanged doubtful looks, then one of them asked, "What's your name, boy?"

"Riley. Riley Sutter."

A soft look settled over both of the men. The smaller of the two men mumbled, "That must be Rus Sutter's boy."

The larger man nodded to his partner, then called to Riley, "Don't worry, son. We'll be inside just a minute or two, and then we'll give you a ride out of here."

"Oh, wow, thanks a million." Riley heaved a great sigh of relief. "I'd really appreciate that."

Meanwhile, Thorpe slipped out the back window, dropped to the ground, and disappeared into the woods.

Preston was in the yard when Ned Buckley and Bill Cherry delivered Riley home to the Upper Place. After an exchange of friendly greetings, they explained to Preston how they had found Riley lost and near tears.

After the men left, Preston made Riley sit down with him on the porch. "So, Mister Woodsman, am

I going to have to buy you a compass and draw you a map of the area?"

"No." Riley frowned. He was in no mood to be teased.

Preston shook his head doubtfully and snickered. "It doesn't reflect well on the Sutter name to have you getting lost."

"I knew where I was."

Preston peered challengingly at Riley. "Then why'd you tell Ned and Bill you were lost?"

Riley realized he was a captive of his own fib, and that it was impossible to play the game both ways. "I told them I was lost because . . . maybe I wasn't exactly sure where I was."

"Oh." Preston guffawed. "You were only half lost."

"Something like that."

"And I suppose you weren't ready to cry, either."

Riley felt like walloping his Pa-Preston, but he suppressed the urge and said, "I may have pouted a little. That's all."

Seven

A week passed before Riley was able to get permission to spend another night in the mountains. The sky was bright and clear when he left the house, and by mid-morning when he arrived at the cave entrance, the day was already hot. He was both pleased and a bit surprised to find the signal rock turned flat side up. This meant Thorpe was inside.

As Riley pulled himself up through the slanted shaft, he began to suspect that something was amiss. The cave was dark and he could hear crickets chirping. He dropped his pack beside the stalactite and lit a match. It burned to his fingertips before he spotted the prone form of his blood brother. "Hey," he called, but did not receive an answer. He struck another match, used it to light a candle, then rushed to where Thorpe lay on his stomach. His head was stuck inside the mouth-shaped crevice.

"You all right?" cried Riley as he tapped Thorpe on the back.

"Ugh." Most of Thorpe's voice was absorbed by the interior of the mountain.

"What's the matter?"

After a pause, Thorpe groaned. "Bad fish, I think."

It took a bit of talking to persuade Thorpe to move, but eventually Riley convinced his ailing blood brother that he would benefit from some sun and fresh air. Reluctantly, Thorpe followed Riley through the tunnel. Almost as soon as they sat down on the hillside, Thorpe vomited.

"Feel better now?"

"Ugh." Thorpe took a swig of water from Riley's canteen, swished it around in his mouth, and spit. "Eewhha. I caught a bass yesterday in the river. I guess I didn't cook it well enough."

"You look kind of green," Riley noted with a grin.

"It's not funny."

"Sorry."

Thorpe took another swig of water and spit. "Say, I want to thank you for saving my hide the other day at the lodge. That was pretty good thinking."

"I figured you heard the truck."

"I heard it. And if it hadn't been for you, they would have caught me for sure."

"I'm just glad it worked."

"It barely worked." Thorpe paused to spit again.

"But then, barely is better than not quite. I owe you one, Riley. Tell me if there's any way I can repay you."

Riley knew this was the opportunity he had been waiting for. "Well, you could tell me about what happened to your mother and why you ran away."

"So, you know about my mother?"

"I sort of know about your mother, but not really," admitted Riley. "I mean, there was a lot of gossip when you disappeared, but at the time I didn't pay much attention."

"People still talking about it?" Thorpe asked worriedly.

"Nah. Not that I've heard."

Thorpe nodded thoughtfully, his blue eyes focused on some invisible point in the distance. With his bad haircut, his ragged clothes, his bare feet, and his sickly complexion, he might have struck an uninformed onlooker as a rather pathetic sight. (To Riley, Thorpe was not even remotely pathetic. To Riley, Thorpe was a brave and resourceful survivor.) After a few minutes he stirred, got to his feet, kicked some dirt and a few leaves over the puddle of vomit, then motioned with his head for Riley to follow. "Come on. Let's go up on the ridge and I'll tell you a sad story."

Thorpe, still a little woozy and moving slower than usual, led Riley to the north end of the ridge, where a flat, sunny rock projected over the western slope. They lay on their stomachs and looked down upon the roof of the gazebo at the rear of the Applegate property.

"Usually when I come up here, even when it's rainy or cold, there's an old lady sitting in that little building."

"That's Phyllis, the judge's wife. She's actually pretty nice. Real easy to talk to."

"She sure likes to sit and watch those springs."

"Praying, I guess. Lisette told me Phyllis was a spiritual."

"Lisette said that?" Thorpe perked with curiosity.

"Yep. They had a conversation about angels or something."

"Oh." Thorpe sighed. Then, pretending that he was only casually interested, he asked, "Is Lisette a spiritual?"

"Maybe. I don't know." Riley shrugged. "She's always been a bit fuzzy."

Thorpe gave Riley a long, curious look, then lifted his gaze high over the expanse of Broken Valley. After a reflective pause, he confessed in a low voice, "I might as well be truthful with you, Riley. Your blood brother is a bastard."

"No you're not," Riley contested.

"Yes I am. I'm a bastard with a capital B."

"I think you're pretty decent."

Thorpe groaned. "I'm a bastard because my real father didn't marry my mother. The dad I grew up with was not actually my dad."

"Oh. That kind of bastard."

"That kind. But I'm glad I am, because the dad I grew up with is the type of no-good bastard you were thinking of."

After a pause, Riley speculated, "So that's why you left home."

"Bingo."

"Who was your real father?"

"I don't know. I never met him. Mom told me once he was a beatnik, but that's about all she'd ever say."

"What's a beatnik?"

"You're on a roll with the questions," Thorpe laughed. "A beatnik is like a hippie. Only older and with shorter hair."

"I think I've heard of them," allowed Riley. "So, what happened? Why'd they put your mom in prison?"

"They put my mother in prison because she blasted my stepdad in the kneecaps with a twelve-gauge."

"She shot him?!"

"Keep your voice down," admonished Thorpe.

"Sorry."

"Yes, she shot him. That's what she did," Thorpe

said in a cool tone. Then some private reflection caused him to snort with amusement. "My stepdad's name is Harry Harkins, and he's a low-down, no-good, bastard bully. He married Mom after I was born. She said he used to be really nice, but I've never seen it. All I know is that he picked on both of us. Sometimes he got rough. Real rough."

Thorpe paused for such a long time that Riley felt a nervous need to fill the gap. "Must have been terrible."

"It wasn't fun," Thorpe replied solemnly, and then again he snorted with amusement. "That's just how it was, until one night Mom told him she was going to shoot him if he ever beat me again. Well, Harry must of forgot. Either that or he didn't believe her. Anyway, it was on a Sunday, in the middle of the afternoon. We were in the living room and he was drunk. For some reason or other he started accusing me of not respecting him. Of course, I told him, that's right, I don't respect you. And then he went berserk and hit me in the face with his fist. The blow knocked me clean back over the sofa."

"Jeez!"

Thorpe's eyes widened and he suddenly started to chuckle with a kind of insane pleasure. "I hardly had time to jump back on my feet, when I look up and Mom is standing there with the shotgun. She just nodded for me to step away, and then she blasted Harry in the knees. As you might imagine, the bastard was shocked. I could tell he wanted to get up and beat both of us, but he couldn't move. He just lay there cussing."

Riley didn't know what was funny about the story, but he could see that Thorpe was pleased to be telling it. "So your dad informed the police and your mom was arrested?"

"Actually, after she shot him, she put the twelve-gauge back in the closet and called the police herself. Then she and I took a walk and we discussed our options."

"Your options?"

"Like what to do if she was sent to prison. It was her idea for me to split. She even gave me money. Lots of it."

"She wanted you to run away?" Riley asked with astonishment.

All traces of humor evaporated from Thorpe's voice and were replaced by bitterness. "She said she couldn't stand the thought of me living another day with that bully."

"But couldn't you have moved in with a cousin or something?"

"Maybe. Maybe not. The problem is, with Mom classified as a criminal, there's a good chance Harry would get custody over me. I wasn't actually adopted, but he was married to Mom, and that makes him my legal guardian."

"Hmm. I see the problem."

Thorpe took a deep breath and rolled over on his back. After a moment, he continued, "So, the plan is to wait until she gets out. Then we're going to move somewhere together."

"Does she know you're living here around Bluff Top?"

"Nah," Thorpe moaned. "I split as soon as I heard Harry was getting out of the hospital. I never got a chance to tell her."

"Oh . . . why don't you just write her a letter?"

Thorpe hesitated before explaining. "I thought about it, and I would like to get her a message because I know she's probably worried, but it's complicated. First, I'd have to get somewhere to mail the letter, and then—what with all the cops, the FBI, and everybody else out looking for me, it would be too tricky. I'm sure they're watching her mail, and I wouldn't want them to be able to trace me back to Bluff County. Then they'd know to look for me here."

"Oh, yeah," Riley moaned thoughtfully. "I see the problem."

"I guess eventually I'll have to find a way to get in

touch with her," mused Thorpe, his voice trailing away.

For a long while the two blood brothers remained on the rock without speaking. In the distance a single turkey buzzard circled over Broken Valley on an updraft. As Riley watched it go round and round, the vague outlines of a daring plan began to sketch itself in the back of his mind.

Part Two

There's a voice in the wilderness crying
A call from the ways untrod.

—FRAGMENT OF OLD HYMN

Eight

Lisette went to the southwest corner of the ornamental garden and climbed the stone wall. There, in the partial shade of a pear tree, she sat admiring the long, bold shape of Bluff Top Ridge. Kissy had gone home for a couple of days and Lisette was now left with plenty of time for ponderous reflection. Beyond the ridge, the blue mountains stretched as far as her eye could see.

Those graceful mountains: Two hundred and fifty million years had passed since the final, catastrophic convulsion of the continental plates gave rise to the Appalachians. That was 238 million years before the emergence of Ramapithecus, the first humanlike primate, and more than 248 million years before the appearance of Homo erectus, our nearest human ancestor. Of course, these measures of time are approximations, rough scientific guesses, and they may be off by a couple of million years. They say the universe is over four and a half billion years old. How do they know?

History, which began with the written word, only came into being six thousand years ago. Before then—before history—time must have enveloped the world like an endless mist. A thousand years must have ticked by like a minute.

It is estimated that three hundred years ago there were just over half a billion humans on the planet. Yet by 1969 as Lisette sat upon the garden wall, there were almost four billion people . . . and counting. (Now, as this story is recorded, there are more than five billion of us. We are a species out of control.)

But Lisette was not thinking of the expanding population, nor was she dwelling on the great age of the mountains. Instead, she was doing what most individuals do, which is to think of the world in terms of their own experience. Lately, her experiences had directed her to contemplate that intangible expanse that is commonly called heaven.

She was glad Kissy had gone home for a few days. Kissy was sweet, and was lots of fun, but she was not very sophisticated when it came to discussing the vagaries of a hidden realm. In fact, she was downright useless when it came to considering the likelihood of guardian angels. Lisette had tried to discuss the topic with Kissy, but her friend just chortled and said, "Gee whiz, I don't know. There might be, but then maybe not."

Since the loss of her parents, and particularly during the weeks following her conversation with Phyllis Applegate, Lisette had been trying to clarify her own concept of heaven. Intellectually, she was befuddled by the esoteric laws that ruled that airy place, but instinctively she believed in its existence. As far as she was concerned, all doubts had been banished by her experience in the woods when she touched the locket and was directed to the idyllic meadow.

As Lisette's eyes wandered along the azimuth of the ridge, she felt the reassuring weight of the necklace resting against her chest. Somehow (without actually defining the feeling in words) she understood that it was a kind of spiritual receptor. It worked for her as a talisman against sorrow. As long as she was wearing the locket, she felt connected to her parents, and as long as she was connected to them, they were not wholly departed from the living.

Lisette had been sitting on the wall for nearly an hour when she heard Riley call her name. "Here," she answered.

"Hey, Mousey," Riley said as he climbed up and

joined his sister. He was the only one who still called her by that name. "Wha'cha thinking about?"

"Things."

"Some-things, any-things, or no-things?"

Lisette smiled. "Invisible things."

Riley skewed his eyebrows in a mockery of deep thought. Then he raised an index finger and opened his mouth to speak. But he did not speak; he just looked at Lisette and closed his mouth.

"What?"

"Nothing." Riley grinned. "It was an invisible thought."

Lisette ignored Riley's stab at humor. There was something she had been meaning to ask her brother. With her eyes fixed on the ridge, she made a sweeping motion with her hand. "What's out there? Why do you keep going away?"

Riley shifted quickly from a joking mood into a serious one. Before replying to Lisette's question, he let a string of thoughts loop through his mind. He knew she was better than average at keeping secrets, and he wanted almost desperately to tell her about Thorpe. Of course he did not; even as he considered the possibility, he knew he was just playing with the idea. A blood pact is something one does not break. Finally he answered, "Just a bunch of snakes, bears, and mosquitoes."

Lisette sensed he was hiding something. "There's a real reason you go away all the time, and I want to know what it is."

Riley sighed before replying, "When I'm in the mountains, the world is mine and I forget all about Mom and Dad."

"Oh," said Lisette. "I wish I could."

Riley was bothered by what he saw as Lisette's attachment to the past. He wished there was a way he could help her let go. "I miss them, too," he acknowledged. "But they're gone, and thinking about them won't bring them back."

"I'm not stupid," Lisette retorted. "I know we can't bring them back."

As Riley stared at Lisette, his mind filled with an image of Thorpe sitting alone in his smoky cave. It reminded him that everyone has their own set of troubles. He moaned, and then in an all-too-rare display of affection for his sister, he slid over and put an arm around her shoulder. "It could be a lot worse than it is, Lisette. At least we have each other. We have Grandma and Pa-Preston. And we have a home."

"I know." Lisette smiled sadly. "It's not like we're complete orphans with no one to watch over us."

"That's right," agreed Riley. "It's not like we're fugitives without a place to go."

• • •

That evening the Applegates came for dinner at the Upper Place. Riley was again surprised by how much he liked the elderly couple. They were skilled conversationalists, and somehow their presence made him feel comfortable and important at the same time. Perhaps it was because they were interesting enough to be interested in young people, or perhaps it was simply because they had a God-given social talent. For whatever reason, it was clear they knew how to draw the best from their company. Lisette seemed to magically snap out of her introspective lost-in-a-cloud mood, Clara started to glow with a certain prim satisfaction, and Preston got so downright cheerful he had three glasses of sherry rather than his usual one.

After dinner Lisette went with Phyllis for a stroll in the garden. Riley joined his grandparents and the judge in the den. It was lying on the floor beside his Pa-Preston that Riley learned of the judge's friendship with the governor of Virginia. Evidently, the two men had known each other since grade school.

"So, old Birdy likes to play poker." Preston was tickled by the information.

"Yes, he does." The judge winked knowingly. "And he doesn't play for pocket change, either."

"I swear," Clara declared. "I suppose the attorney general gambles as well."

"Oh, don't be an old biddy," Preston poohed at his wife.

Judge Applegate adopted an innocent expression and avoided eye contact with Clara.

At this point Riley sat up and cleared his throat. "Excuse me, sir. But can't the governor pardon criminals?"

The judge's expression went from innocent to owlish. "That would depend entirely upon the facts."

"But he could if he wanted to?"

"Yes, Riley." Judge Applegate nodded sagaciously. "It is within the governor's power to pardon criminals. Why do you ask?"

"Oh, no reason." Riley shrugged nonchalantly. "I was just wondering."

Lisette felt an almost giddy anticipation as she guided Phyllis through the arbor and into the garden. There were many things on her mind (of the invisible variety), and she could hardly wait to discuss them with her sensitive guest. As they sat on the bench, Lisette remarked humbly, "It's not as exciting as the bubbling springs, but it's usually quiet."

"Oh, I think it's just divine," trilled Phyllis.

Lisette felt suddenly bashful about addressing the subject on her mind. Instead, she patted the bench and said, "Pa-Preston made this during the Depression."

"It's held up very well."

Lisette nodded again and blushed. Her head was filled with a chorus of loud thoughts, but she simply could not find any words to express herself.

Phyllis, being a shrewd reader of moods, had a notion as to what was on Lisette's mind. "And you, how are you holding up?"

"I'm okay."

"I see you're still wearing your mother's necklace."

Shyly, Lisette offered, "I only take it off to bathe."

Phyllis's eyes sparkled knowingly. "Tell me, dear, have you seen any signs of your guardian angel?"

It was the subject Lisette had been hoping to discuss, and who better to discuss it with than someone who told stories of trips to heaven and hidden voices. She knew Phyllis would understand. "Yes," she said with alacrity. "I had a sign the other day."

Phyllis's face became an instrument for listening.

Lisette began by explaining how she and Kissy had been bored on the porch, then she chronicled their hike into the forest, told of being lost, and described how she had touched the locket and been led along an invisible path to the picture-book meadow. "At first I didn't understand what had happened," Lisette added at the end of her story. "But then the more I thought about it, the more I knew I'd been guided through the woods."

Phyllis exhaled slowly and stared into the reflecting pool. It was obvious she was considering the nuances of Lisette's tale. Soon her eyes widened, then blinked with insight. "Yes," she decreed. "It sounds very much like a guardian angel to me."

Lisette felt the chill of gooseflesh. "But where was the angel? I didn't see anything."

Phyllis smiled knowingly at Lisette. "But you felt it. You knew where to go. You must remember, whenever one deals with a guardian angel, there is a certain ephemeral quality to the whole affair."

"Ephemeral?"

"They come and go quickly. They vanish," Phyllis explained.

"How?" Lisette was wide-eyed with curiosity. "Where do they vanish to?"

Phyllis hemmed. "I'll tell you what I know. Guardian angels are made essentially of spirit, and the spirit likes to move freely. Where it goes, or how, I'm not sure. But I do know that the spirit is not overly fond of attention. It likes to hide."

"So guardian angels are invisible? They don't have bodies?"

Phyllis flashed another knowing smile. "Well, yes. And no. As I believe I told you before, sometimes the spirit will associate closely with a particular personality—a person—and it will guide that person to action. In this way the guardian angel does take form."

"You mean, like . . . it overtakes somebody?"

"No. *Overtake* is too strong a word. What it does is coach the spirit of someone who is already inclined to do good to begin with, prompting that person to perform certain acts." Phyllis paused before adding, "Because of this, guardian angels are never obvious. It is extremely rare to ever see one in action."

"You mean, people do see them?"

"They've been seen in the past. But these days, with all the confusion in the world, hardly one person in a million will ever see an angel at work."

"But it's possible?" Lisette asked hopefully.

"Yes, of course it's possible," Phyllis concurred. "But even if by some wild chance you did see your guardian angel, it would be the briefest of brief glimpses, and you might not realize it was an angel."

"Oh," Lisette said dreamily, her mind already beginning to tell her that she was that one in a million who would see.

Night had invaded the mountains by the time Lisette and Phyllis left the garden and started for the front porch, where Clara had promised dessert. As they stepped around the corner of the house and entered the front yard, they both halted in their tracks. A great, luminous moon had risen over the valley, and there was not a cloud in the sky to lessen its brilliance. Down below, the river shimmered like a long, golden snake. "Heavens!" Phyllis shrieked with all the exuberant joy of a child. "Lisette, look at the river!"

"I know, it sparkles. That's how it got its name."

Just then the front door opened and Riley appeared on the porch. When he spotted Lisette and Phyllis standing in the yard, he turned back into the hallway and hollered, "Okay, Grandma! They're out. here. Y'all come on now."

Moments later, everyone present that night at the Upper Place was standing alongside the porch rail, eating watermelon and spitting seeds in the yard. Everyone, that is, except Thorpe Greenwood. Heartwrenching but true: He was lying in the tall grass at the edge of the field below the yard. His gaze was focused primarily upon Lisette, and he was wishing like hell he could have a slice of watermelon, too.

Nine

After several days of imagining angels and pondering the movement of spirits through the world, Lisette's mind grew weary from the challenge. After all, she was not a mental gymnast. She was a young teen trying to put her life in perspective.

Speaking of perspective ... after looking at the books that her grandmother had given her to read, Lisette was of the opinion that Clara could use a good dose of the stuff herself. Lisette understood her grandmother's intentions were all good and well, but it was apparent that Clara was peculiarly out of touch with the times. One of the books, published in South Carolina in 1930, was entitled *The Difference Between a Gal and a Lady*. It was purportedly about social etiquette, but it read more like a list of moral clichés. Yet *The Difference Between a Gal and a Lady* seemed sensible next to the other book Clara had given her.

This one, a dog-eared paperback printed in England, was called *How to Say No to Boys*. It was illustrated with such corny, old-fashioned drawings that Lisette wondered if it had been intended as a satire.

Lisette was considerate by nature, and so she did not complain when she returned the books to Clara. She merely handed them over and said, "Thank you."

"I hope you weren't shocked."

"No, I wasn't shocked."

"But you did read them, didn't you?"

"Yes, Grandma," replied Lisette. "And now I know that if a gentleman plays in his pockets in my presence, I should waste no time in finding an excuse to leave the room."

Clara was not sure, but she thought she detected a hint of sarcasm in Lisette's voice.

Rather than sarcastic, Lisette was feeling awkward. To begin with, there was no boy in her life to say no to, and furthermore, if one did come along, she could not imagine treating him in the coy and tactical manner suggested by Clara's books.

Lisette was generally relieved a few days later when Kissy returned to the Upper Place. With Kissy around there was no time to worry about boys, or confuse oneself with thoughts of the invisible world. Kissy was a summertime gal, and her idea of a profound question was "What's for supper?"

During these early weeks of July as Kissy and

Lisette frittered away the days with idle games and laughter, Riley escaped into the mountains as often as possible. Under Thorpe's master tutelage, he continued to train in the arts of stealth and survival. Among other things, he learned how to make numerous birdcalls, how to skin and cook a squirrel, how to sit perfectly still for an hour, and how to accurately operate a slingshot. Although his skills with a slingshot never approached Thorpe's genius, he did progress to the point where he could usually hit the trunk of a tree at thirty yards.

With each journey that Riley made into Thorpe's world—some for just a day to deliver supplies, others lasting through long nights of talk—the bond between the boys was strengthened. Bit by bit, situation by situation, Riley learned to read Thorpe's changeable moods and accept his upswings with his downs. (Not to suggest that Thorpe was manic; it was simply that he did his thinking in isolation and was vulnerable to intense extremes.) For his part, Thorpe gradually began to reveal more of his true self. As Riley eventually realized, the brusque exterior of Thorpe's personality was more a product of his environment than a reflection of his real nature. Basically, Thorpe was kind and giving, and had he been living in gentler circumstances, he surely would not have developed such a sharp edge.

In spite of his growing openness, there was one dimension of his inner life that Thorpe tried to conceal from Riley. That dimension existed near his heart, and had everything to do with Lisette. Riley was not fooled. He recognized a pattern in the way Thorpe regularly asked supposedly innocent questions about his sister, then listened intently to the answers. Although Riley had never had a crush on a girl before, he suspected that this is what was going on with his blood brother. It did not seem like a bad thing, and he was delighted to provide whatever information he could.

There was one more issue on the burner during those first weeks of July 1969. It was a delicate issue, involving a radical plan that Riley had proposed. Initially he could not get Thorpe to even discuss the plan, but after much persistence, he finally got him to consider the proposal.

And then, soon after the notion of getting a message to his imprisoned mother had taken root in his mind, Thorpe became its most staunch supporter. Granted, it was a proposal in want of development, a proposal that lacked a plan, but it was a good idea, which ultimately called for action.

"You'll have to get to Petersburg. That's where the Virgina State Women's Correctional Facility is located."

"Bus, I reckon."

"I've got money for tickets."

"I'll get a schedule from Clear Glen. I've never taken a Trailways before."

"You'll have to pretend you're someone else. If you use your real name, they might trace you back to Bluff County."

"How about Hector Gonzales? I've always liked that name."

"Don't be ridiculous. Besides, it has to be a name that Mom would recognize."

"Sorry. Do you know what you want me to tell her?"

"Hmm. I'll have to think about that."

The boys were well ahead of themselves. It would not be until the middle of August before they enacted their plan, and presently, the calendar was still hanging on July.

July 20, 1969, was a Sunday. After nearly a week of rainy, overcast days, the sun broke through the clouds in the morning and rose brightly into the sky. It was a spectacular day in Bluff County; hot, yet with a breeze. It was also a day destined to loom large in the annals of science.

Science: that field of systematic investigation into the general laws that rule this universe. Science: that rapidly evolving creature that supercedes our culture's ability to adapt. A century before, the world had no telephones, no airplanes, no gasoline engines . . . yet on this given Sunday in July '69, two humans stepped out of a lunar module, walked on the surface of the moon, and were seen on television by millions of people.

On average (it varies due to the moon's elliptical orbit), the distance from earth to the moon is 238,857 miles. Quite a trip. If you were to ride your bicycle a hundred miles a day (possible, but not likely), it would take you more than thirteen years to ride to the moon and back. The spacecraft Apollo 11 made the journey in little more than a week.

But back to the spectacular day that dawned over Bluff County. Lisette recognized it for exactly what it was: a call for her and Kissy to get on their bicycles and ride to the Sparkling River.

"There's a spot near Jagged Gap with rapids to wade in," she told her friend, "and flat rocks for sitting in the sun."

Kissy was easily persuaded. "I'm game," she chirped.

They left the house just before noon. The first two miles were mostly downhill, and the girls spent more time braking than they did pedaling. When they reached the heart of the valley, where the little white-clapboard Methodist church sat at a fork in the road, they halted at the edge of the shaded parking lot. At a word from Lisette, they got off their bicycles and plopped down under a massive old oak tree.

For several minutes they sat without speaking, listening to the breeze whispering through the leafy boughs above them. No special sensitivity was required for Kissy to know Lisette had something serious on her mind; that was made plain by the fraught and faraway expression on Lisette's pretty face.

Eventually Lisette's features drew back into focus and she shared a bit of what she was thinking. "I haven't been to church since the funeral."

Kissy did not know what to say, so she groaned.

"It's okay. I'm used to it now," Lisette replied to Kissy's sounding of concern. "What I really miss are the hymns."

"Can't you go back anytime you want?"

Although Kissy's question was perfectly reasonable, Lisette gave her a long, dubious look. "I could go back . . . but I'm sure the hymns wouldn't sound the same without Mom."

And then, as if on cue (Lisette would later wonder if it was mere coincidence or an instance of divine synchronicity), the church vibrated with the muffled sounds of song. She leaned forward and cocked an ear to listen. Although many of the words were lost in the breeze, she was able to discern a few phrases.

There's a voice in the wilderness crying. A call from the ways untrod. Something unclear, then: *. . . a high-way for our God.* More lost words, then: *. . . val-leys shall be exalted. The lofty hills . . .*

"Recognize that one?" Kissy grinned slyly.

"No, never heard it before," Lisette mumbled as she rose to her feet. "Come on. Let's go swimming."

As the girls were mounting their bicycles, the faint traces of a final refrain wafted past them. *There's a voice in the wilderness crying.*

The girls were red-faced and puffing when they reached the end of the trail to the river. They leaned their bicycles against a tree, then hurried to a sunny spot by the water. There they removed their shoes and outer garments, which they threw on the shore in a disorderly pile. They already had on their bathing suits. Lisette took the necklace from around her neck and set it on the sand beside their clothes.

Kissy stuck an investigative toe into the swiftly running water and cried, "Oooh! That's chilly."

Lisette rolled her eyes. "You're supposed to plunge."

Kissy nodded challengingly at the water. "I don't see you plunging anywhere."

Lisette grimaced, took a fortifying breath, then charged into the river.

"Well," wondered Kissy. "How is it?"

Exaggerating only slightly, Lisette reported, "It's nice once you get in."

Kissy yelped before taking the plunge.

After a few minutes in the cool, embracing water, the girls climbed onto a rock in the middle of the river and stretched out to warm themselves in the sun. They had been lying on the rock long enough for their swimsuits to dry when Kissy suddenly whispered, "Oh, no."

"What?" Lisette asked languidly. Her face was turned to the sun and her eyes were closed.

"I think I see trouble."

"What?" Lisette asked again, but then she heard voices on the shore and understood Kissy's alarm. When she glanced over, her muscles tensed. It was Boone Jett and Mike Mackenzie, two of the county's more irascible teenagers. Boone's black truck was parked at the end of the trail. Each boy held a beer, and both were leering at the girls. "Just ignore them," Lisette advised. "Maybe they'll go away."

It was soon apparent this tactic would not succeed.

"What've we got here?" shouted Boone. He was the older and more obnoxious of the two.

"Looks like a couple of mermaids," Mike observed loudly.

"Could be, but probably not," Boone carped as he bent over and fondled a blouse. "These look like clothes. And mermaids don't wear clothes."

"You're right," Mike conceded. "Must not be mermaids."

Boone held the blouse up for inspection and laughed. "This is pretty. I wonder if it would fit me?"

Surprising both herself and Lisette, Kissy whirled toward the riverbank and screamed, "Don't you dare!"

"Ah, listen," Boone snickered. "She's upset."

Undaunted by the bullying, Kissy persisted. "You leave those clothes alone or I'm . . . I'm turning you in to the law."

"Shh," shushed Lisette.

Boone was tickled by Kissy's threat. He picked up the clothes and tossed them toward the woods. "What clothes?"

"You rat!" Kissy cried.

"Hush, Kissy," commanded Lisette. "You'll aggravate them."

It was too late. Boone shared a dark look with Mike, then glared back at the girls. Kissy and Lisette sat frozen with fear, wondering what he might do. It was apparent that he was considering the same thing. Tension rippled through the air; the situation was about to turn nasty. Boone shook his head, and then, speaking loudly for the benefit of the girls, he suggested, "Mike, what do you say we swim out there and see what's under those bathing suits?"

Mike sat down and began removing his shoes. "I am kinda hot."

"Crap," Kissy groaned. "What are we going to do now?"

"Oh, Lord." Lisette trembled. "Please help."

Boone set his beer down and quickly unbuttoned his shirt. He was fumbling with his belt buckle, when he suddenly jerked to the side and cried out in pain.

"What?" Mike jumped to his feet, then immediately staggered backward and screamed.

Kissy and Lisette exchanged astonished looks. It appeared as if Lisette's prayer had been answered.

Boone put a hand to his cheek, where a trickle of blood had begun to flow. Just as he turned to examine the woods to his left, he was struck squarely in the forehead with a rock. "What the hell?" he cried as he reeled backward. Then *thwack*: Another rock hit him in the chest. He crossed his arms in front of his face. "Mike, what is it?"

Thwack: A rock hit Mike's right kneecap. "I don't know, but I'm out of here," he blurted as he bolted for the truck.

Boone directed a final, confused glance in the direction from which the rocks seemed to be coming, then raced to catch up with his sidekick. As he ran, a rock went zinging through the air and stung his buttocks.

The girls sat stunned as Boone's black truck exploded into gear and lurched backward up the trail. Lisette's mind was too flushed with relief for her to analyze what had happened, but her heart knew to be grateful to someone . . . or something.

Tires screeched on the paved road and a straining engine raced south toward Jagged Gap. "Quick," ordered Lisette. "Let's go before they come back."

Kissy was in the water and swimming toward shore before Lisette even got to the word *back.*

They speedily retrieved and donned their clothes. Kissy moved like a flash. She was already pedaling up the trail before Lisette could tie her shoes. Lisette ran to catch up, but halfway to her bicycle, she stopped and peered into the woods at the spot from which the rocks had projected. She gasped. Suspended deep in the greenery, made faint by heavy shade, was the face of a young boy. Or at least she thought she saw a face. It seemed to disappear in the blink of an eye.

The girls had just ridden past the church parking lot when Lisette stomped back on her pedal and skidded to a halt. "Oh no, my necklace. Kissy, I left my necklace by the river."

"I'm not going back there."

"We have to."

"Now?"

"Please."

Kissy's frown suggested determined resistance. Then suddenly she had an alternate idea. "Let's just go on to the Upper Place and get your Pa-Preston to drive us back."

"Good thinking," agreed Lisette, who wasted no time in resuming the journey home.

Ten
—

On Monday the barometer fell as another low-pressure system drifted into Bluff County. Except for the sunny Sunday when the astronauts had walked on the moon, the weather was just like the week before. The daytime skies were brooding and overcast, and at night it rained.

Thorpe Greenwood was lying in darkness on the granite floor of his solution cave. It was the fourth successive night of rain. He was hungry, yet he did not feel like building a fire and cooking a pot of beans. He was tired of beans. Earlier in the day he had eaten five soggy crackers and two green apples.

Something was wrong with Thorpe, yet it was not his stomach. His malaise was much larger than his stomach. It felt as if his entire chest cavity was hollow. Not only was he tired of beans, he was tired of his day-to-day survival routine. Rather than getting easier with practice, it was becoming an increasingly difficult challenge. Since the near-disaster on his last trip to the Stills Bend Hunt Club lodge, he had been reluctant to venture into unoccupied homes and onto farms for fresh supplies. As a consequence his diet was suffering. If it were not for Riley arriving with the occasional meal, the situation would have been much worse.

Although Thorpe blamed the rain for making him depressed, he knew there was another, more dominant factor contributing to his sense of ill-being. But on that, he put no blame. He just remained on the cold, hard floor of his cave, listening to the incessant song of the crickets, wondering about that factor's all-pervasive power. It seemed crazy to him that he could not cease thinking about someone he had seen only three times in his entire life. If that was how love worked, then love was cruel.

"How could this have happened?" Thorpe's voice echoed softly through the stone chamber. "Did it strike me when I heard her singing? Or did it creep up slowly?"

At the same time Thorpe was lying in the darkness on the unforgiving floor of his cave, Lisette was in her bed, surrounded by pillows, staring blankly at the gray skies outside the east window of her bedroom. Although there was a great contrast in the comfort of their physical surroundings, and though the causes of their respective depressions were not the same, she was feeling no less blue than Thorpe.

It was four in the afternoon. Lisette had been in bed since shortly after twelve, when Melinda Kidder had come to retrieve Kissy. By Lisette's own calculations, ninety-nine hours had now passed since she removed the necklace from around her neck and placed it on the riverbank by her clothes. In her mind, that was ninety-nine hours without grace.

Over and over in her mind she replayed the scene at the river. First her terror, then her profound relief as Boone Jett and Mike Mackenzie retreated under a barrage of stones. Now, in retrospect, the whole sequence of events seemed like a fleeting dream. Had she *really* seen a face floating in the greenery?

Lisette did not know what to believe. She only knew that there was a mystery that needed solving. Someone or something had protected her . . . but could the face have actually been the face of her guardian angel?

And the necklace: Where was the necklace? She could vividly recall every move that Boone and Mike had made that day, and she was certain they did not take the necklace. Yet for three frustrating hours she and Kissy and Preston had scoured the riverbank. Surely the necklace had not vanished into thin air.

Clara was deeply disturbed by Lisette's recent turn of mind. Initially, back in the spring, it seemed to her as if Lisette had adjusted fairly well to the tragic loss of her parents. But now, after this latest brouhaha over the necklace, Clara was no longer so confident about her granddaughter's recovery.

"What?" Lisette replied blandly to the rap at her door.

"I've brought you some cookies."

"Okay, come in."

Clara set the cookies on the desk by the southwest window and went to sit on the foot of Lisette's canopied bed. "Are you feeling any better?"

Lisette grimaced, then dismissed the question with a curt roll of the eyes.

Clara sighed compassionately. "Sweetheart, I know it was precious because it belonged to your mother. But it was only a necklace. You can't let it destroy you."

Lisette glared fiercely at Clara. "You don't understand."

"I might if you told me."

"Well, I'm not going to tell you," Lisette snapped. "I don't feel like talking about it. Okay?"

"Fine," Clara agreed quickly. She was too concerned for Lisette's psychological health to take offense at her rude behavior. She moved as if to rise from the bed, then paused. "I was on the phone with Phyllis Applegate a little while ago."

Some of the hardness left Lisette's face.

"I told her you were feeling a bit under the weather."

"Why'd you say that?" Lisette asked in a caustic tone.

Now it was Clara's turn to glare, although she did so with compassionate restraint. "Because I didn't think I should say you had taken to your bed in a foul and miserable mood."

Lisette nodded deferentially. Clara had a point.

"She invited you for lunch tomorrow. If you decide to go, call her this afternoon."

Lisette's eyebrows quivered with interest, but she did not reply.

Clara turned at the door and nodded toward the desk. "Don't forget your cookies."

It was still drizzling on Friday morning when Riley pushed through the thicket of mountain laurel near the entrance to his blood brother's hidden home. He was pleased to see the signal rock pointing skyward, but a moment later when he reached the end of the tunnel and looked up, he was disappointed at the sight of darkness. His first thought was, I hope Thorpe hasn't gone and eaten another bad fish.

But as Riley was soon to discover, Thorpe had not eaten anything at all. When Riley handed him the quart of milk he had to offer, Thorpe demonstrated the effects of his fasting by downing the whole thing in a single, greedy gulp.

"Brrrp. Thanks. I needed that."

"Next time I'll bring a whole cow."

"I'd probably eat it if you did." Thorpe grinned. He was glad for the company, and was feeling suddenly rejuvenated by the milk. "Is it still raining?"

"Of course."

"Hold on. I'll cozy this place up." Thorpe moved confidently through the darkness and took a handful of kindling from the rick of wood by the far wall.

After a flame was established and the cave flickered into view, Riley proudly told Thorpe, "I got a bus schedule. There's a Trailways that leaves out of Clear Glen at seven thirty-five on Sunday mornings. It gets to Richmond at nine, and then there's a bus every hour to Petersburg."

"Good work. How much are the tickets?"

"Twenty-eight dollars round trip."

"A bargain. I'll give you eighty."

"Eighty? That's a lot, isn't it?"

"Not really. You're going to have to take a taxi

from the bus station, and we don't know far it is to the penitentiary. Anyway, I have over eight hundred dollars."

"Eight hundred! Your mom gave you eight hundred dollars?"

Thorpe ignored Riley's reaction. "So, when will you make the trip? Maybe Sunday next week?"

"No, I can't go then. That's August third, my birthday, and Pa-Preston is taking me to Baltimore to see the Orioles play the Red Sox."

"The Orioles. You lucky dog. Congratulations."

"Thanks. . . . So, anyway, I should be able to go the Sunday after that, on the tenth . . . that is, if I can figure out how to get to Clear Glen by seven thirty-five in the morning."

"Hmm." Thorpe considered for a moment. "Probably have to make a night hike through Broken Valley. I can lead you as far as the old mill where Fast Creek goes over the falls. It can't be more than two or three miles into town from there."

"Good. Okay. Let's make it the tenth. I won't be able to come a lot before then. You know . . . I kind of have to build up some good time around the house. Have you thought any more about what you want me to tell your mom?"

"Yes. I think I just want you to tell her I'm alive, that I miss her, and that I still have all my teeth."

A short time later the sun sent the clouds packing and the sky turned a bright baby blue. But by then the boys were engaged in a closely contested, double-deck game of War and were unaware the rain had stopped. They were also unaware that not far west of the cave, on the other side of the ridge, Phyllis Applegate was greeting Lisette at the door to her home.

Although Lisette did her best to muster a smile when Phyllis welcomed her into the foyer, Phyllis could see she was suffering beneath her thin facade. She already knew from Clara that Lisette had lost the necklace.

A linen-draped table awaited them in the court-yard. It was appointed with artfully folded napkins, wildflowers, and fine china. The judge was somewhere in hiding, and would not be joining the girls.

During the passage of their chicken-salad lunch, Lisette sat in her chair like a discouraged mouse and let Phyllis do most of the talking. She was not intending to be sullen; it was just that her spirits were so low she could not think of anything to say.

Later, after strawberry shortcakes with whipped cream, Phyllis sliced through the fog and asked Lisette directly, "What could possibly be making you so sad?"

"I ah . . ." Lisette mumbled, then abruptly burst

into tears. "I lost the necklace. Mom had it for fifteen years, and I lost it in two lousy months."

"Now, now. Don't cry," Phyllis said soothingly. "Tell me what happened."

Lisette sniffled, then began recanting the pertinent events of July twentieth. She told of the threat Boone and Mike had posed, of the unexpected and timely barrage of flying rocks that had appeared, and lastly, of leaving the necklace on the rocky riverbank.

Phyllis sat perfectly still until the tale was told. Then she shrugged and asked rhetorically, "Who really knows what is and is not possible? After all, we are only human beings."

Lisette used a napkin to blow her nose. She was not sure she understood what Phyllis was suggesting. Nevertheless, she agreed. "Yes. Just humans."

"There is so much that happens in this universe which is beyond our capacity for comprehension," Phyllis noted philosophically. "Are you with me?"

"Yes," replied Lisette. "I mean, no. Not really."

"What I mean to say is maybe it was just a boy in the woods by the river that day. But also, maybe it was your guardian angel. And if it was—which, since he protected you, I believe it was—then maybe he took the necklace." Phyllis paused for an instant to reflect. "Maybe he took it to use for some special purpose which neither you nor I can quite imagine."

A portion of Lisette's intellect wondered if Phyllis's mind was all there, yet everything in her heart and the rest of her mind answered the contrary: If anything, Phyllis Applegate was perfectly sane.

"Remember, Lisette, *your* guardian angel is always on *your* side. They do what they do with love."

Lisette touched her chest where the locket should have been and moaned.

"Keep pondering, dear," Phyllis said encouragingly. "I'm sure it will all become clear to you before long."

Eleven

The month of August started as the month of July had ended, with rain.

Although it was not raining early on Sunday, August third, as Riley and Preston climbed into the Buick for the three-hour drive to Baltimore, the skies were ominous. They encountered a brief shower in Culpeper, then passed through a heavy mist around Washington, D.C. When they crossed into Maryland, the sun was out. It was not bright, and it was not pretty, but it was clement enough to play baseball in Memorial Stadium.

It was a slow game. Frank Robinson hit a solo shot over the left-field wall in the bottom of the fourth. That was it for runs. At least the Orioles won.

"I had a pretty good time," Riley said cheerfully when they finally found the Buick.

"I could have sworn we parked on the other side," grumbled Preston. His feet were tired, and he was still scratching at the mustard and relish stain on the seat of his pants.

"Sorry about the hot dog," Riley said for the fifth time. "I didn't know you were going to sit down."

During the following week (another wet, clammy week just like the previous three weeks) Riley stayed close to home and paid particular attention to behaving thoughtfully. It was all part of his good-credit strategy. He wanted to maximize his chances of getting permission to depart on August ninth for two nights in the mountains.

In preparation for his trip to the prison in Petersburg, Riley spent half an hour of each day scripting the name Mark Rawlings. Thorpe had a cousin by that name from Elizabeth City, North Carolina, and it was the name Riley would be using at the guard gate. It was Thorpe's idea for him to practice writing the name. Being the cautious creature Thorpe was, he wanted to eliminate the possibility of a sharp-eyed guard noticing that Riley—or rather, Mark—was unfamiliar with his own name. As an added precaution against any tricky questions, Thorpe instructed Riley to study a map of North Carolina.

With each day and night that brought the weekend closer, Riley's reservations about his pending mission increased tenfold. The tight scheduling, the false identity, the prospect of being frisked at the gate . . . it made him feel like some kind of calculating spy. He did recall that his great-great-great-great-grandfather Rufus J. Sutter had actually been a spy, but the thought provided little solace. After all, Rufus was a full-grown man when he served in the American Revolution against the British, and Riley had only been thirteen for less than a week.

Why did I ever open my big mouth? Riley wondered.

Saturday finally arrived. Again the skies were overcast, but it wasn't raining when Riley left the Upper Place at noon. Not yet.

Thorpe surprised him at the twin boulders near the base of the hill where the cave was hidden. "Mark Rawlings," he whispered as he appeared out of nowhere.

Riley, already in a state of nervous agitation, gasped for air. "You nearly scared me to death."

"Wouldn't want to do that to my top messenger," Thorpe replied amicably. "Here. Let me carry your bag."

Clearly, Thorpe was in one of his upswing moods. There was a big grin on his face and a sparkle in his eye. Riley had never seen him quite so happy or excited. "Did you take a bath?"

"Yep. Washed my clothes, too."

"You're not planning to come with me, are you?"

A twitch of remorse flittered over Thorpe's face, then quickly disappeared in a smile. "Nah. I just thought it was time to get clean again. Remember you said it would help my rash if I scrubbed it good with soap?"

"Yes."

"Well, I did, and it helped a lot."

Riley considered asking about the nasty and persistent boil on the back of Thorpe's neck, but he was afraid that speaking of it might affect his blood brother's upswing mood. Instead, he handed Thorpe his bag and said, "I'm glad it helped. Getting cleaned up seems to agree with you."

According to Riley's pocket watch, it was eight forty-seven in the evening when the boys sat down to a feast of peanut butter sandwiches and rabbit stew. Afterward, at nine-twelve, Thorpe ceremoniously packed his pipe with the last available pinch of tobacco and lit it with a stick from the fire. He looked kindly upon Riley, blew a smoke ring, then professed warmly, "I've never had a blood brother before, so I really wasn't sure what to expect, but it's a brave thing you're about to do for Mom and me. I'm not sure if I'll ever be able to repay you."

Riley was suddenly reminded of why he had opened his big mouth and committed himself to this venture. In all the world, he had no better friend than Thorpe. "You've already repaid me."

"How's that?"

"Well . . ." Riley hesitated, then laughed. "You taught me how to sneak around like a thief."

Thorpe shook his head and grinned. "So, what's the time?"

Speaking slowly at first, then hurrying his words for the sake of accuracy, Riley reported, "It is exactly nine-fifteen on the dot."

By midnight the easy conviviality of the evening had given way to a mounting tension. The final hour and a half before their departure passed especially slowly. At twelve-thirty, Thorpe extracted a wad of bills from a deep niche in the wall and gave Riley eighty dollars. "Put twenty in each shoe, then carry the rest in your front pocket."

"Do you think someone will try to rob me?" Riley stammered.

"No," Thorpe said with an exasperated sigh. "It's just the way you're supposed to travel."

"Sorry. I didn't know that."

"Now you do. What time is it?"

"Twelve thirty-eight."

"Put your extra clothes in this bag. I'll carry it."

"Right. Anything else?"

"Just wait . . . that's all we do now. Are you nervous?"

"Nah," Riley said bravely. "Just a little excited."

A hard rain was falling at two A.M. when the boys emerged from their solution cave. It was just what Thorpe had hoped would not happen. Heavy, black skies obscured the waning moon, which he had been counting on to illuminate the way, and the infirm soil beneath their feet grew more treacherous with each additional raindrop. They would have to hurry if they were going to travel the length of Broken Valley before dawn.

The mountains sang with the sound of a million leaves being pelted by rain. The boys climbed the ridge, then descended the rocky slope behind the Applegates' house. There they picked up Fast Creek, which they followed into the dense valley.

In spite of the many impediments before them, the two blood brothers moved swiftly and steadily toward their goal. Riley, who by any standard was no slouch in the woods, could hardly believe Thorpe's apparently magical instincts for reading the terrain and anticipating obstacles in the darkness. Time and time again—always without hesitation—he managed to pick the best route around a thicket, the shortest cut through a gulley, or the most expedient path across a dale. And though Thorpe did this through periods of driving rain, and through a valley where many day-time hikers were easily foiled, not once in four hours did he guide them awry.

The rain began to taper off at six in the morning, and by six-thirty it had stopped completely. A half-hour later, right on schedule, the boys arrived at the old mill near the road into town. This left just enough time for Riley to change into his traveling clothes, walk the three miles into Clear Glen, buy a ticket at the Esso station, then wait for the bus. They were hop-ing luck would prevent anyone who knew him from driving by while he stood at the station.

"It was smart of you to bring socks," said Thorpe as he handed Riley his clothes.

"Wish I'd brought another pair of shoes. These are soaked."

"They'll dry out," noted Thorpe, turning away while Riley changed his pants. "So, this is it."

"It's it, all right," Riley adjoined somewhat ner-vously. "Are you sure you don't want me to tell your mom where you're living?"

"I'm sure. Her life must be hard enough as it is. She'd just worry if she knew I was living in a cave."

It occurred to Riley that Nina Greenwood's life in prison could not be much harder than Thorpe's precarious existence on the outside. "I'll tell her you're doing fine."

"Thanks." Thorpe nodded solemnly. "So, I'll be here at dark tonight, waiting right behind that tree."

"Okay. See ya." Riley reached to shake Thorpe's hand, then stepped into the road. He had progressed about ten feet when Thorpe called, "One more thing."

"What?"

"Don't forget to tip the taxi-cab driver."

"How much?"

"Two dollars ought to do it."

Riley had proceeded for approximately another thirty yards when Thorpe called again, "Tell Mom I love her."

Riley turned to wave, but there was no one in sight.

The bus was ten minutes late. Riley was surprised to find that only six of the forty-two available seats were occupied. He sat near the front with his face glued to the window, where for the first hour of his journey he stared attentively at every detail in the passing landscape. Here and there a passenger got on, or off, at one of the many small towns en route.

Although it was all very novel and exciting for Riley, he was exhausted from hiking all night and sleep soon overtook him.

There were so many weirdos hanging around the bus station in Richmond that Riley wondered if they were having a convention. He purchased his ticket to Petersburg, and then—ever conscious of the twenty-dollar bills in his wet shoes, and doing his damndest to think and be invisible—he ensconced himself on a bench near the front door, where he anxiously awaited the next southbound bus.

Meanwhile, back at the Upper Place, Kissy and Lisette were admiring themselves in the hall mirror. Both were dressed for the eleven o'clock service at the Sparkling River Valley Methodist Church. They were waiting for Clara and Preston, who had decided at the last minute to accompany the girls.

As Clara rationalized to Preston, "We might as well attend. Otherwise one of us has to drive them down, then drive back and pick them up."

Preston was amenable. "Who knows? A spot of preaching might do us old sinners some good."

"I don't suppose it could hurt," agreed Clara. "Besides, I think it'll please Lisette to have us with her."

The cold truth was that Lisette did not care whether her grandparents attended church or not. Although her condition had improved slightly after her curious conversation with Phyllis Applegate, she was still depressed over losing the locket. This was day twenty-one without that precious object, and she had reached the point where the actions of others bore little significance on her state of mind. Today all she really knew for certain was that she was in the mood to sing a hymn.

Their late entrance into the church engendered many raised brows and stunned smiles. Lisette took the lead, and with Kissy, Clara, and Preston trailing closely on her heels, she marched boldy to the front of the sanctuary and sat down in what had once been her and Alison's regular pew.

The service began with organ chimes, which were followed by the Doxology. Then the Invocation, the Prayer of Confession, and the Prayer of Pardon. Afterward came a long, particularly didactic sermon, during which Preston fidgeted constantly and Clara kept nudging him to sit still. Finally a hymn was announced. Number 453. When Lisette found the selection in her hymnal, she felt a twinge of disappointment. It was a hymn she had never sung before. During the first verse her voice was small and tentative. But then in the second verse, she caught the rhythm of the music and let her voice rise into the song. And as her voice lifted, her spirits began to soar. It seemed as if the hymn was speaking directly to her: *When shad-ows haunt the qui-et room . . . Help us to un-der-stand . . . That Thou are with us through the gloom . . . To hold us by the hand. And though we*

do not al-ways see . . . The ho-ly an-gels near . . . O
may we trust our-selves to Thee . . . Nor have one fool-
ish fear.

If we as individuals could be in more than one place
at a time, we would see that life is rich with poignant
coincidences. But we are limited; we can only be
where we are. Thus we rarely know of the many con-
current and meaningful events taking place just
around the bend.

Sunday, August 10, 1969, was a fertile day for con-
current events. Just as Riley's southbound connection
to Petersburg pulled into the station, and as Lisette
was singing the words "And though we do not always
see, the holy angels near," Thorpe Greenwood was
huddled in the darkness of his cave, crying without
restraint. He was hungry. He was wet. He missed his
mother. He was tired of scratching to survive. After
nearly fourteen months in the shadows of Bluff Top,
the emotional deprivations of his isolated life had finally gotten to him. He did not know where he
would find the will to carry on.

Yet Thorpe was made of substantial stuff. He had
not come this far without learning that his inner re-
sources would rally to meet his needs.

Soon he stopped crying, and when he did, he
found the will to carry on. The will was born of a rea-

son, and that reason was embodied in an object not far from hand.

He flicked on a flashlight and reached into his worn and tattered satchel. Then, for the umpteenth time in twenty-one days, he opened the clasp on the small gold locket and read: *Such is our love that even the angels in heaven are impressed.*

Twelve

The Virginia State Women's Correctional Facility, Camp Thirty-three, was located eleven miles south-west of the bus station in Petersburg. Wayne Beaman, Riley's affable taxi driver, had this to say: "It's not too bad, I don't reckon. I knew a gal who went in there all stupid and mean, and a couple years later when I saw her, she had a high-school degree and was acting real civilized." Wayne laughed heartily. "So, Mark, who you going to visit? Your momma?"

"A cousin," Riley lied. "I'm from Elizabeth City. That's in North Carolina."

Wayne nodded. He seemed to know better than to pry. A few minutes later he turned left into a paved parking lot. "Here's the joint. That'll be five dollars."

Riley gave him seven. "The extra two are for you."

Wayne was surprised and pleased. "Thank you, Mr.

Rawlings. I always said the folks from North Carolina had good manners. You want me to wait for you?"

"Would you? I might be in there a couple of hours."

"Might as well wait. I don't see any fares hollering for a ride back into town."

Until now, Riley had remained fairly relaxed about his mission, but when he stepped out of the taxi and turned to face the prison, his heart began to race. It was an intimidating sight for any individual, and especially so for one as young and free as Riley. Two chain-link fences, set six feet apart, surrounded the compound. The outer fence was ten feet tall and topped with barbed wire. The interior fence, topped with a forbidding coil of razor wire, was even taller. Every seventy-five yards stood a guard tower. Riley was afraid to study the towers too closely. He did not want to draw unnecessary attention to himself.

By the time he reached the guardhouse at the main gate, he had actually begun to entertain the thought of turning around. Then suddenly the door opened to reveal a rather pleasant-looking woman in a dark blue uniform. She smiled when she saw his sigh of relief. Riley stammered that he had come to visit Nina Greenwood. The woman checked a list, then directed him toward the visitors center.

He passed through two electronically operated gates before entering the visitors center. Here he was greeted by a huge, dour-looking woman with a mustache. She handed him a form, which she instructed him to read and then sign. (She did not notice how easily he scripted his name.) When he returned the form, she pointed to an adjoining room and told him to go sit down. Four men and one woman glanced up as Riley entered the cheerless waiting room. He sat, bowed his head, and did not make eye contact with any of the other visitors.

Eventually, a male guard wearing thick glasses appeared at the waiting room door and called, "Mark Rawlings." Riley arose and followed him into the lobby. The guard startled him by asking, "You carrying any weapons?"

Riley quite adamantly shook his head.

The bespectacled guard laughed. "Didn't think so. Still, I have to frisk you before we enter. Regulations."

After a perfunctory pat-down, the guard unlocked a steel door and led Riley into a long, windowless corridor. At the end of the corridor was another steel door, which the guard also unlocked. Then they stepped into a small, enclosed park area. In the park were a dozen picnic tables, half of which were occupied by prisoners and their guests. The prisoners were

recognizable by their garb; all wore dark blue dunga-
rees and light blue cotton shirts. Riley felt remiss
when he noticed that many of them had received
gifts of flowers and food from their visitors.

"Greenwood will be here in a moment," said the
guard. "Since you're a juvenile, I have to keep you in
view. Regulations. Just make yourself comfortable. I'll
be here when you're ready to go."

"Thanks." Riley swallowed nervously.

The instant Nina Greenwood stepped through a door
on the far side of the park, Riley knew it was
Thorpe's mother. She had the same coal-black hair,
and there was no mistaking the high cheekbones.
Riley waved. She studied him uncertainly for a moment, then began moving toward the table where he
was waiting.

Riley was temporarily discombobulated by
the woman who sat across from him. She had
Thorpe's eyes, and he had not expected her to be so
beautiful.

"Hi, Mark," Nina said softly. In spite of the circumstances, there was an aura of dignity surrounding
her. The number 91968309 was stitched over her
right breast pocket.

"I'm not Mark Rawlings," Riley whispered.

"I don't suppose you are." Nina stared directly at

the young imposter. "Mark Rawlings must be nineteen or twenty by now."

"Oh." Riley blushed. "Thorpe didn't tell me that."

"Thorpe?" Nina's voice broke with anxious concern. "Have you seen Thorpe?"

"Yes. He told me to tell you he's doing fine. He still has all his teeth and everything."

"Thorpe. Thank God. When did you see him last?"

"This morning. He wanted me to—"

"Where? Where did you see him?"

Riley bit his bottom lip. "He said not to tell you where."

"Why?" Nina asked with sharp concern. "Is he in trouble?"

"No. He's fine. Honest, he is. He's just afraid you'll worry if you know how—where he's living."

As Nina paused to absorb what she was hearing, Riley could see lines of anguish in her beautiful face. It was clear that thinking of Thorpe caused her pain. "How is he?"

Riley thought about Thorpe's rash, his boil, and his rapidly declining weight. Then he lied. "He's fine . . . happy as a clam."

Riley's eyes may have betrayed his doubts, but if they did, Nina pretended not to notice. "Who are you?" she asked.

"My name is Riley. I'm Thorpe's friend," Riley said

with a certain pride, then added, "Actually, we're blood brothers."

"Blood brothers," Nina repeated with an understanding smile. Something in her smile reminded Riley of his own mother, and he sighed sadly. Suddenly Nina reached over the table to touch his folded hands. "It's nice to meet you, Riley. It was good of you to come here. I'm glad Thorpe has such a brave friend."

"He's the brave one." Riley blushed.

Nina's smile melded into a thoughtful gaze. "I take it he is hiding somewhere, and you're helping him."

Riley confirmed her speculation with a nod.

"When will you see him again?"

"Tonight, when I get back to . . . when I get back."

"I have some important information I'd like you to give Thorpe. Will you do that?"

"Sure. Yes, ma'am. Absolutely. That's what I'm here for."

Riley felt like he was walking on air as he left the prison. When Wayne saw his face he laughed. "You look much improved from earlier. Did someone tell you where the loot was hidden?"

"Nah." Riley grinned. "Better than loot."

"I'm mighty glad to hear that, Mark. So, back to the bus station?"

"That's right, Wayne. And step on it, will ya. I've got good news to deliver."

Nearly four hours later as the big Trailways rolled out of the flat, Tidewater region of Virginia and entered the eastern foothills of the Blue Ridge, Riley was still buzzing with an irrepressible joy. The trip had exceeded all hopes. Not only had the mission gone according to script, but a marvelous new twist had been written into the plot. Repeatedly, as if there were a tape in his head running on a short loop, Riley reviewed the facts: Nina Greenwood had obtained a divorce from Harry Harkins, which meant that he was no longer Thorpe's legal guardian, which meant that Thorpe could come out of hiding. Nina said her lawyer in Greenville could arrange for Thorpe to live with a foster family until she was released, which meant that maybe—if justice was to be done, and Riley was going to lobby diligently to see that it was—Thorpe could live with the Sutters at the Upper Place.

Riley was so elated by the promise of the day, he felt he might float out of the bus window and fly the rest of the way back to Clear Glen.

But sometimes, as Riley was soon to be reminded, life has a way of popping one's balloon.

• • •

That Sunday at dinner, Preston offered to treat Kissy, Lisette, and Clara to dessert at the DairyFreeze in Clear Glen. The offer was received with enthusiasm. Afterward, on the way home, Preston pulled into the Esso station to fill his big Buick with gas. He just happened to be standing by the pump, speaking with Puddin Wright, when the Trailways stopped at the curb. Riley (his luck could not have been worse if he had planned it) did not spot the car until it was too late. The instant he stepped off the bus, Preston looked his way.

"Riley?"

"Pa-Preston."

"Clara, look."

Clara turned to the right. "Oh, Lord. What's he done now?"

When they got home to the Upper Place, Riley tried to explain that he had just gone for a joyride to Culpeper and back. Even if his grandparents had believed him—which they did not—his claim did nothing to mitigate their fury. They decried that they had been deceived, their leniency taken for granted. "Is this our reward for allowing you to spend two nights in the mountains? Is this the way you repay our trust?"

"I'm sorry."

"You are sorry, young man," Clara retorted angrily. "And you will remain sorry until you learn to demonstrate some respect for your Pa-Preston and me."

After confabulating in private, Clara and Preston fashioned a sentence to fit the crime. "Riley, you are restricted to your room for ten days and ten nights. We will bring you your meals, but you are not to leave the room except to use the toilet."

"No ifs, ands, or buts about it, either," added Preston.

Thorpe arrived at the old mill an hour before twilight and ensconced himself in a thicket near the tree where he was to meet Riley. He was excited by the prospect of hearing news of his mother, and his spirits, which had been so low earlier in the day, were on the rise.

Slowly, darkness fell over the mountains and the stars appeared. He should be here any minute now, thought Thorpe. Any minute.

An hour later, Thorpe began to have doubts about whether Riley would come. An hour after that, he succumbed to his doubts and began to worry if Riley was safe. Perhaps the bus had gotten a flat tire. Maybe there had been an accident on the road. Perhaps there had been a problem at the prison. Maybe . . . oh hell, he did not know what to think.

Still, he kept hoping against the evidence that Riley would arrive at any moment.

Finally, close to midnight, after four long hours of wishful thinking, Thorpe accepted that Riley was not going to keep their appointment by the tree. For Thorpe, it was one more sad fact to carry in his large basket of troubles. With a heavy heart and a head full of unanswered questions, he began the return trek to his lonely cave. At least the route was well established. This was his fourth trip through Broken Valley in less than twenty-four hours.

At three-thirty that morning when Thorpe wearily hoisted himself out of the tunnel and sprawled out on the stone floor of his cave, his blood brother was lying wide awake in his bed at the Upper Place. Riley should have been long gone in dreamland. His body was tired from the adventures of the past twenty-four hours, yet his mind would not allow him the luxury of sleep. It had too many decisions to make. And not one of them, it seemed, could be made without a price.

If he told his grandparents the truth, he would be breaking his pact with Thorpe. If he ignored their commands and went to deliver the news to Thorpe, then he jeopardized the chances of their later considering the idea of sponsoring Thorpe for foster care. If he waited out the ten days . . . well, poor Thorpe.

While Riley stared into the darkness and weighed one option against the other, it began to rain again.

It was still raining on Tuesday night when Lisette got up from her desk and went to the east window of her bedroom. By now the incessant patter of rain on the slate roof above had become a maddening background drone. Rat-a-tat, rat-a-tat. It was enough to drive even a peaceful soul into a troubled funk.

Lisette was so worn out from being depressed, she was almost happy again by default. She rubbed a circle of condensation from the window, and was thinking of nothing in particular when she heard a noise below. Craning her neck, she looked down as Riley leapt from the house into the boughs of a nearby oak tree.

Riley hurried through the drenching night as fast as he could propel himself. After two days of internment, he had finally decided that Thorpe deserved to hear his mother's news sooner than later. Actually, he had not made a rational decision but rather had given into a compulsion to act. Thorpe had to be told. It was as simple as that. If he got caught . . . well, he would deal with that devil when it showed its face.

The route from the Upper Place to Thorpe's hidden cave was not a leisurely stroll in the best of conditions, and on this dark night with the driving rain, it was a veritable morass of soggy, slippery, unstable footholds. By the time Riley scrambled up the hillside toward the tunnel entrance, he was a muddy mess.

"Thorpe," he started calling before he reached the slanted shaft that opened into the residential chamber. "Thorpe. Wake up. Where are you? I have good news for you, buddy."

Chirping crickets was the response. The cave was as dark as the inside of an eight ball.

"Ah, come on. Where are you?" Riley shouted with frustration.

Although he had no way of knowing it, the answer to his cry was the Sparkling River Valley.

After subsisting for several days on meager rations from a perilously low food supply, Thorpe had devoured the last morsel of his fodder. And so tonight, desperate with hunger, he had gone to raid a couple of farms in the valley. He would have to take care to eradicate his footprints, but otherwise, the rain provided excellent cover for this endeavor.

Riley found a flashlight, and he found paper, but he could not find a pen or a pencil anywhere. Finally, urgently, he took a burned stick from the cold fire pit and employed it as a writing implement. It was a crude tool, which he had to stop and sharpen after every word, yet it allowed him to leave a hurried message: *Tues. nite. Your mother fine. Got good news. But I'm in trouble at home. Return when I can. Hang on. R.*

Thirteen

As a matter of record: In the summer of 1969, beginning in mid-July and continuing into the third week of August, rain fell at least once a day, every day, somewhere in Virginia. During this gloomy spell more than a foot of rain fell over the Blue Ridge Mountains, and everyone in Bluff County had begun living in a moldy, languid sort of dream. There were a few maverick thinkers who said the bad weather was caused by the astronauts walking on the moon, but generally, this theory was not taken seriously.

In the early hours before dawn on Wednesday, Riley returned to the Upper Place. He stashed his wet and mud-stained clothes in the field beyond the garden wall (they would have been hard to explain), then climbed quietly back through his bedroom window.

At noon there was a knock at his door. He assumed it was his grandmother delivering lunch. "Yes. Come in."

Lisette entered and, without a word of greeting, plopped down on the bed. Riley was sitting in a rocking chair by the south window. She stuck one pillow behind her head, then wrapped her arms around a second pillow.

"Make yourself comfortable," Riley bid with a wan smile.

Lisette returned his smile in kind. "Believe I will."

After an elongated pause during which neither sibling had anything to say, Riley remarked, "This weather sucks. It makes me wish I was a frog."

"You kind of look like a frog," observed Lisette.

"Thank you, Mousey."

"You're welcome. So, Riley, where'd you go last night?"

"What?"

"You heard me," Lisette said in a cool tone.

Riley averted his eyes, turning to look out the window. He knew that when Lisette took a cool tone she was not to be easily put off. "Do Grandma and Pa-Preston know?"

"I didn't tell them. So, where'd you go?"

"Oh, I took a walk," Riley lied. "I was feeling cooped up and I wanted to stretch my legs."

Lisette knew Riley too well to fall for such a lame fib. It was apparent he was hiding something. But what? Why would he keep it a secret about where he went, and why would he continue to go there? It made no sense. Unless . . . suddenly she had a hunch. She threw off the pillow she was holding and sat forward. If the hunch was true, it answered many of the questions that she had been asking herself lately. "There's someone living out there!" she blurted excitedly. "That's it. That's why you keep going into the mountains."

Riley turned back to his sister with a doubtful frown. "That's got to be the dumbest idea I've heard all summer. I go into the mountains because I like the mountains. And because when I'm out there, I don't have to put up with stupid people who can't mind their own business."

Lisette was not misled by Riley's histrionics. Indeed, they only served to confirm her supposition. She wondered why she had not discerned the truth earlier. Coolly, she stated the facts: "There's a boy out there. He has black hair and he throws rocks at people."

Riley wrinkled his brow in an attempt to strengthen his frown. It only served to make him look less convincing. "I do wish I knew what you were talking about."

"You know exactly what I'm talking about." Lisette

peered steadily at Riley. "I know you know because I can see it in your eyes. Besides, it explains everything."

Riley feigned incredulity.

"Who is he?" Lisette insisted.

"Who is who?"

"Ah, come on, Riley. You know who. The guy who saved Kissy and me from those bullies at the river. Does he have my necklace?"

Riley lifted himself purposively from the rocker, stomped across the room, and stood face to face with Lisette. "Mousey, you've got a real problem. All the thinking you've been doing about invisible things has bent your imagination. I'm sure that's why you've been so down in the dumps lately."

Lisette just smiled. "When you see him again, tell him I really appreciate what he did. But I want my necklace back."

"What are you talking about?" Riley shouted with desperation.

"No need to raise your voice," Lisette said with a smirk as she hopped from the bed and headed for the door.

"Listen." Riley grabbed her by the elbow. His voice now carried the elements of a plea. "If there was something I could tell you, I would. But I can't. Okay? So don't start spreading any false rumors."

Lisette's smile was forgiving. As far as she was concerned, the core of a mystery had been revealed. And with the revelation, she realized there was someone out there who knew about her ... someone with a handsome face ... someone who had defended her against harm. She remembered Phyllis Applegate saying that guardian angels do what they do with love. The thought caused her heart to tremor. "Why won't you tell me?"

Riley's shoulders slumped with defeat. "If I tell you why, then I've already told you too much. But, Lisette, I swear to you, I don't know a thing about your necklace. Nothing. I swear."

Lisette sensed that Riley was telling the truth about her necklace. It suddenly occurred to her that the situation was more complicated than she had guessed. "Riley, are you in some kind of trouble?"

"No." Riley hung his head. "Aside from being restricted to my bedroom, I'm not in trouble."

That weekend it rained over most of the continental East Coast. The inclement weather did not appear to dampen the spirits of the four hundred thousand rock fans gathered in Bethel, New York, for the Woodstock festival, but it did annoy the hell out of most Virginia farmers. They watched helplessly as tons and tons of topsoil eroded from their inundated fields. Hardly a one of them suspected that it would get worse before it got better.

On Saturday, August 16, 1969, Hurricane Camille reared her ugly head in the Gulf of Mexico. She was a mighty creature, with winds surpassing those of all storms in recent memory. She started east toward the Florida panhandle, then turned abruptly north toward the mouth of the Mississippi River. Officials advised residents to evacuate the coastal areas of the state. Those who were prudent heeded the warning, yet, as is often the case in the face of an unseen danger, there was a cocky contigent of individuals who ignored the threat and remained in their houses. Some of them even threw parties to celebrate the coming storm.

The next evening, August 17, as hordes of burnt-out hippies straggled away from Max Yasgur's farm in upstate New York, the town of Gulfport, Mississippi, was wracked by the high winds and surging tides kicked up by Camille. In many of the buildings that collapsed, the impudent individuals who had refused to evacuate paid for their temerity with their lives.

The National Weather Bureau predicted that Camille would begin to dissipate as soon as she made landfall. They were technically correct—her winds did drop from 160 mph to 120 mph—but they were essentially wrong. During the next two days and nights, in an awesome display of natural power, Camille cut a swath across the southern United

States that made Sherman's March seem incidental by comparison.

By Tuesday afternoon, when Camille arrived in Virginia, her winds had diminished as predicted, but she had lost none of her ability to produce rain. In a freak meteorological occurrence, she stalled while trying to pass over the eastern lip of the Blue Ridge Mountains. It was a most unfortunate event for anyone living on low ground. In a deluge that lasted for two hundred and seventy minutes without surcease, Camille sucked clouds in from over the Atlantic and dumped more than twenty inches of rain onto the already-saturated valleys and spongy hills of Bluff County. (Consider that one inch of rain falling on one acre of land equals 226,512 pounds of water. That converts to 27,143 gallons. Multiplying this by twenty, one learns that more than half a million gallons of water per acre fell upon Bluff County in approximately four and a half hours. The precipitation was more severe in nearby Nelson County, where the National Climatic Data Center estimated that twenty-seven inches of rain had fallen during the same period.) Sheds, barns, trailers, and houses were ripped from their foundations. Trees toppled, bridges washed away, and anyone who could do so headed for higher ground. It was the worst natural disaster ever to hit the Old Dominion.

From the Sutters' vantage point at the Upper Place, Camille did not seem particularly devastating. She wielded no lightning. She did not roar. From their point of view, she was little more than a notably windy and enduring rainstorm. Preston was inclined to agree with his grandson, who said, "I've seen worse, except for the rain."

Rain. That was Camille's signature. Hours and hours of rain.

Unfortunately, everyone in Bluff County did not enjoy the Sutters' elevated vantage point. In the Sparkling River Valley, people perceived the storm for what it was: a monster. They had no delusions in the valley. Down there the Sparkling River had transformed the world into a disturbed sea of rising water.

The next morning, the first thing the sun did after tearing through the clouds was reach into Riley's bedroom and tickle him awake. This was Day Ten of his restriction, and the way he saw it, penance had been paid. He jumped from bed, dressed quickly, and then (without deigning to inform his grandparents of his departure) he darted from the house.

All around him the world had changed. Bushes were splayed, smaller plants uprooted, and the hay in the fields lay flat. By the time Riley entered the bruised and battered woods on the north slope of the plateau, he had begun to develop a belated respect for Camille. It was a respect that expanded immensely when he reached the gulley where he usually crossed over to Gallihugh Mountain. It was no longer a gulley; it was a gorge filled with a torrent of muddy water.

After whispering the imprecation "Hell or high water, here I go," Riley stepped boldly into the runoff. The current tugged him sharply southward. Twice he stumbled and was almost pulled under. But he was in a serious mood, and the resistance just made him more determined to gain the far bank.

When he finally did drag himself up onto the far bank and glance forward, his newfound respect for Camille turned to awe. The entire lower third of Gallihugh Mountain had been denuded by a landslide.

Riley did not have time to survey the destruction. After a couple of quick, investigative prods into the mangled mass of earth and trees blocking his path, he determined that he should seek an alternate route to the cave. He recrossed the flooded gulley, then ran due west along the north rim of the wooded canyon. He figured he would turn north again at the base of Bluff Top, then come down on his target from above.

As Riley hurried through the damaged forest, his thoughts ran ahead to Thorpe. He could hardly wait to give him the news about his mother's divorce.

Maybe, he thought excitedly, Thorpe would return with him today. And the sooner the better, he reflected. Although he had informed Nina Greenwood that her son was doing fine, he knew it was not the truth. Thorpe's physical health was fading fast, and his mental equanimity was suffering from too many long, lonely nights in the cave.

When Riley arrived at what he thought was the vicinity of the hidden cave, he was perturbed that he could not immediately locate the target hill.

Perhaps I'm in the wrong area, he thought as he surveyed his surroundings. Let me see now. I'm approaching from the opposite direction. Maybe I've gone too far north. Anyway, there should be a familiar landmark somewhere.

After several minutes of confusion, Riley saw the set of twin boulders that told him he had overshot his mark by a hundred yards. He turned and backtracked. At first he saw nothing to alarm him, but then—in an agonizing flash—he understood why he had not identified his target hill on the first pass. There had been another landslide. The top third of the hill was naked with mud.

Riley was frozen with dread as he viewed the mass of wet earth and shattered trees jumbled around the foot of the hill. For several seconds he simply could not move, but then he broke free of his fear and scrambled over the wall of destruction. Frantically, he clawed his way upward. When he reached the elevation where the mountain laurel and the ledge should have been, his heart nearly exploded with anguish. There was no mountain laurel. There was no ledge.

He screamed and looked around. Where was the entrance hole?

Suddenly, he felt a sense of relief. He was mistaken about the hill. It was not the right one.

This time, calmly, he studied the landmarks. Back to the west was the ridge. Slightly north and to the east he could see Gallihugh Mountain rising through the trees. Below and to the south a hundred yards were the twin boulders. The target hill should be somewhere . . . about . . . here.

Again he felt a numbing cold in his heart. He looked down. Mixed in the mud at his feet were branches of broken mountain laurel. "Oh, God. Please, no. Make it not so!"

He wanted to believe Thorpe had spent the night elsewhere, but he knew differently. The cave was shelter from a storm. The cave was home. The cave was a trap.

On his knees digging . . . scooping and tearing at the soil with his hands. He found a stick and jabbed it repeatedly into the wet earth. It snapped, useless against the packed soil at the base of the ledge.

"A shovel!" he screamed. "I got to get a shovel."

Suddenly he was running downhill. Out of control. He tripped and tumbled. He got up and climbed over the wall of wet earth and shattered trees.

Then he remembered the crevice in the cave. *He has air.*

He charged heedlessly through the woods, heading straight for Gallihugh Mountain. He recalled the landslide blocking his path ahead, but he did not bother to turn. It was the shortest route home. He would crawl through the crap if he had to.

Running madly. Mind crying. Got to get a shovel fast!

Part Three

From this valley they say you are going,
When you go, may your darling go, too?
Would you leave her behind unprotected
When she loves no other but you?

—"The Red River Valley,"
POPULAR FOLK SONG

Fourteen

Thorpe was dreaming of a hot breakfast served to him in a soft bed when he was awoken by a strange and ominous sound. At the heart of the sound was a low-frequency rumble that permeated the walls and floor of the cave. It was louder than a jet plane during takeoff.

He sat up, every fiber in his body attuned to the sound. He could feel the rumbling in his bones. The softer, sharper edges of the sound seemed to be coming through the tunnel.

Soon the strange sound began to subside. It ended with a final slurping noise that echoed throughout the cave.

Thorpe sat still as a stone, afraid to move and upset the silent balance. Earthquake, he thought initially. And then, aided more by instinct than logic, he began to suspect that there had been a landslide. For the longest while he remained as a stone. He was in no rush to verify his suspicion.

Eventually he took a flashlight and peered down the slanted shaft. At the bottom of the shaft he saw a dark, viscous mud that completely obscured the tunnel. It was a horrible sight.

He emptied his bucket of tools, then used the container to scoop the slimy substance from the shaft. As he scooped, the mud continued to rise. He accelerated the pace of his activity. When the bucket was full, he hoisted it from the shaft, carted it across the cave, then dumped its ugly contents through the mouth of the crevice. He could hear the discarded muck splattering and slapping against rock as it descended toward hell.

It was hard work, bending over and lifting the heavy weight. He repeated the process twenty-two times before ultimately accepting that he was involved in a futile endeavor. The slime was rising faster than he could scoop and dump.

He sat down on the bucket to contemplate the situation. From everything he could determine, the circumstances were dire and essentially devoid of hope. In the final analysis he concluded that he would probably die. That was the thing about Thorpe. Life had turned him into a realist.

He began to consider death, first as a general concept, then as a personal experience. Taking nothing for granted, he tried to imagine what it would actually feel like to pass over to the other side. He was not imagining death in theory (as even the most timid among us are apt to do occasionally), he was imagining it in real, honest time.

It was not long before he made a distinction between the act of dying and the fact of being dead. Although one clearly led to the other, he discerned a critical difference. In his mind, the act of dying was the lesser evil: It was a relatively brief physical process, and it would get him out of the jam he was in. But being dead—well, that was an immutable condition that took away everything. It meant he would never see his mother again. Being dead precluded his ever thanking Riley for all his brave support. It meant his heart would never quiver again at the sweet sound of Lisette Sutter's voice.

After considering all this, Thorpe decided that being dead was a condition to avoid at any cost.

He took stock of his fodder. Two carrots. A hardboiled egg. Six crackers. One pitiful-looking apple. No tobacco.

After a while it occurred to him that he was already in a tomb. For some convoluted psychological reason, he was humored by the thought. He threw back his head and laughed in the face of the Maker.

It was not much of a laugh. It quickly disintegrated into a kind of haunted simper.

The first thing Riley noticed when he awoke was the smell of antiseptic. Then he realized he was dry. He wanted to ignore his senses and return to the peaceful womb of sleep, but a throbbing pain drew him out and he opened his eyes.

"Hi, Riley."

"Mousey?" Riley was lost.

"You're in the hospital."

"What?"

"You've been in a coma."

"Me?"

"Yes, you." Lisette nodded. "I'll be right back. I promised Grandma I'd tell her as soon as you woke up."

The world was a fuzzy place. He hardly had time to accept that he was in a hospital bed before the door swung open and Clara floated across the room. Preston was on her heels, with Lisette right behind him, and behind her a uniformed nurse.

"You're going to be all right," Clara gushed.

"Boy's got pluck. I've always told you that," mumbled Preston.

"How do you feel?" Clara lay a hand on Riley's forehead.

"Sleepy."

"Your leg is going to heal just fine," said Preston.

"My leg?"

"It's broken," offered Lisette.

Riley glanced down and saw that his left leg was in a cast. "What? How'd that happen?"

"Let him be for a moment," ordered the nurse. "I'll go get Doctor Kimmel."

Riley's head began to clear, and soon he was able to recall climbing onto the unstable mound of earth and trees at the base of Gallihugh Mountain. Vaguely, he remembered traveling across the tricky surface of the jumbled mass . . . then abruptly he was watching the sky recede, while behind and beneath him the world rapidly sank. That was about all he could remember. Preston had to tell him the rest of what had happened during the past two days.

Bill Cherry, who had the maintenance contract for Long View Cemetery, had gone up to Gallihugh Mountain on Thursday morning to see what damage Camille had wrought upon the graveyard. It was mostly undisturbed; the landslide had occurred below the burial grounds. Fortunately, curiosity had drawn Bill over the hill for a closer look at the dislodged debris. By a stroke of luck, he peered at the right spot and saw a body protruding from the jumbled mass.

Riley was unconscious when Bill got to him and freed his leg from between two fallen trees. He had remained unconscious during the trip to the hospital, throughout surgery, and during that night and the following day.

Now it was Friday evening and Riley could hardly believe what he was hearing.

"You are a lucky boy," said Doctor Kimmel.

"I'm lucky?" Riley whispered in disbelief.

"Lucky enough. You've had a concussion, and from the look of the bruise, I'd say you are lucky it didn't hemorrhage."

"He's got a hard head," remarked Clara.

"Fortunately, it runs in the family," mumbled Preston.

Doctor Kimmel bent to inspect the pupils of Riley's eyes. "I'll want to monitor you for a few days. But if all goes well, you should be home by Tuesday."

"And my leg?" Riley could barely issue the words. "When will I walk again?"

"The cast will come off in a month. I expect you to be walking by the end of September."

Thorpe did not know how much time had passed. It felt like a couple of days, but it might have been more. Time really was not the important issue.

His mind was unraveling. He had considered every aspect of his situation at least a hundred times, and now his thoughts were turning in on him and going nowhere. Basically, they boiled down to a flip-flop. On the outside, Riley was his only hope. On the inside, there was the one option of going through the crevice. As of yet, he was reluctant to even acknowledge the inside option.

It was with bitter irony that he recalled his words to Riley on the night they made their blood pact: *I don't care if I belly up and die of rot—but you have to swear you'll never, ever dream of telling a soul you even think I live anywhere near Bluff County.*

"Riley," Thorpe's anguished voice echoed through the dark cave. "What did you learn from my mother? What was the good news you were going to tell me?"

Finally, the decision settled over him and he accepted the inside option. He flicked on a flashlight and stared at the mouth of the crevice. The face he had drawn on the wall was smudged and faded, and now it suggested something more akin to a demon than a man. He understood that when he entered the crevice he would be committing himself to an abyss of no return.

Of course, considering the alternative of expiring in a cave with a community of jittery crickets, he also understood it was a commitment that was already made.

Slowly, solemnly, he ate everything in his fodder. Then he gathered all the available rope and tied the different sections into a single line. He estimated the line was fifty or sixty feet long. He tied one end of it to a bundle of firewood. Then he grabbed both flashlights. One he put in his hip pocket, the other he jammed under his belt against his stomach. He took Lisette's necklace from his satchel and dropped it in a front pocket. He thought about the wad of money hidden in its niche. It seemed irrelevant, and he decided to leave it behind.

After a final, sentimental look around his humble home, he squirmed feet first into the demon's mouth.

Fifteen

By Sunday night Riley's mood had turned so foul that Clara wondered if the mental darkness was a symptom of his concussion. She had known her grandson to be aloof and secretive on occasion, but it was unlike him to be completely rude. She tried not to take it personally, but her patience was wearing thin. First Lisette had been depressed for a month (thank goodness her disposition had finally improved), and now Riley seemed determined to pick up where she left off. What was a grandmother to do?

The only remotely pleasant sign from Riley came at nine o'clock when hospital visiting hours were over and his family arose to depart.

"Thanks for coming," he said with a small smile. "Would someone cut the lights out?"

"Yes, Riley."

"See you tomorrow."

"Cheer up, son."

Riley felt as if every hope and every dream he had
ever believed in were all for naught. The future lay in
front of him like a torture chamber. He had only
himself to blame—if he had delivered Nina Greenwood's message a day earlier, Thorpe would now be
wandering around free. Perhaps he would even be living at the Upper Place. He would have a life. But
that was not the case, and a thousand times Riley
asked himself: Why did I wait in my room like a self-
ish, yellow-bellied coward? Why did I let this happen
to the one person in the world who needed my help?

Riley knew he would never forgive himself for the
fatal lapse in time. Though he dared not imagine the
details, he knew there was no fate worse than being
buried alive.

Dear God, he prayed, if there is a heaven, please
take my blood brother swiftly.

Although the date mattered not a whit to Thorpe, it
was Sunday night when he exercised his only option
and entered the demon's mouth. He knew from previous inspections that the gap opened over a cylindri-
cal shaft that dropped through solid rock. The cross
section of the descending tube was about eighteen
inches wide, and as it dropped, it curved inward

under the cave. Because of the curve, he had never been able to see farther than twenty feet down.

He propped himself in the top of the cylinder, drew the rope through the crevice, then yanked it past himself until the bundle of wood was wedged securely against the inner wall of the cave. After it was set, he slid the rope under his left leg, lay it over his right leg, and pulled it across his chest and past his right shoulder. Then he shrank away from the wall of rock and began to rappel his way into whatever subterranean gallery awaited him.

As he made his descent into the dark, unknown world, he regretted the twenty-two buckets of slime he had dumped into the tube. Eventually, though, as the inward curve of the passageway became more pronounced, he left most of the slime behind and forgot about this minor inconvenience.

At about forty feet down he encountered a crag, which jabbed into his buttocks and back as he passed over it. Below the crag the tube widened and he lost contact with the wall. He tightened his legs and one arm around the rope, grabbed a flashlight, and peered below. He was suspended in the ceiling of a small room. It was a relatively easy, fifteen-foot slide to the floor. The space was about ten feet wide and twenty feet long, with one end of the chamber occupied by a heap of large stones. At first he was relieved to rest his burning hands and stand again on a firm surface, but when he glanced around without seeing a continuance of the passageway, his relief quickly became a thing of the past.

"Why has everything gone wrong in my life?" he screamed. "What did I do to deserve this?"

He considered attempting the rugged climb back up to where he started from, but even as he considered, he knew that struggle would accomplish absolutely nothing.

Soon the devil began to dance with his mind. Die here? Die there? What does it matter? What does anything matter? I might as well make a noose right now and hang myself. In a couple of years I'll just be an old skeleton.

"Thanks a lot, Lord."

After a long, intensely troubled while, Thorpe escaped into the mercy of sleep. Ah . . . so tranquil and soothing. That warm sun in the bright blue sky. He was naked, standing on the banks of the Sparkling River. He heard a shrill cry and he looked up to see a hawk circling overhead. When the hawk saw him looking, it dipped a shoulder and dove toward earth. Then someone said, "Sorry," and Thorpe turned just as Riley's head popped from beneath the surface of the river. Thorpe wanted to thank him for some cookies he had left at the cave, yet when he tried to speak his lips would not part. An object crashed in the water and Riley disappeared. It was the hawk. No, it was his mother in a canoe. She smiled and waved as she floated past him. He wanted to go to her. Then he remembered he was naked, and he whirled around to look for his clothes. All he saw was an old shoe. He turned back to tell his mother he still had all his teeth, but she was gone. He heard the hawk cry again, and when he looked up he realized he was sitting in a tree. Then he heard a soprano voice and he felt a gush of great happiness sweep through him. Lisette was perched on a branch above him. She smiled down at him and started singing: *From this valley they say you are going. When you go, may your darling go, too? Would you leave her behind unprotected, when she loves no other but you?*

Thorpe awoke in the darkness, the image of Lisette lingering sweetly in the back of his mind. Then his senses reminded him of where he was. He flung out his arms, as if to swat back reality, and screamed, "This place shall not be my grave!"

Empowered by an incited will, Thorpe turned his attention to the heap of stones at the west end of the chamber. He knew air was entering the room from somewhere, and this was the logical place to look. It was the only place to look.

He propped the flashlight up so that it illuminated

the pile of stones, then he began to disassemble the mound with a fury. Many of the rocks were the size of basketballs, or larger. It was a strenuous task moving them one by one to the opposite end of the room, yet he was driven by desperation and he did not shrink from the job. The more stones he removed without encountering a wall, the more inspired he became with the prospect of surviving. And thus, sweating and grunting like a single-minded gnome, he maintained his assault on the dwindling pile.

Hour upon hour. First a dent, then a recess that became a cavity in the pile. All the while the beam from his flashlight grew increasingly pallid. Finally it faded into an ineffectual hint of light and died. Fortunately, he had the second flashlight. He activated it and resumed his persistent attack.

He was not thinking. He was simply moving the next stone when he suddenly broke through. He grabbed the flashlight and poked his head into the opening. The sight almost took his breath away: He was gazing down into an underworld so vast it swallowed the beam of his flashlight as if it were a filament penetrating a lake. It was the most amazing place Thorpe had ever seen, and for several minutes as he peered awestruck into the immense chasm, he forgot all about his mortal plight.

From ceiling to floor the cavern was at least a hundred feet high, and from all he could see by the beam of his flashlight, it was endless. How many years—a hundred, a thousand, a million, a hundred million— had this cave been waiting for Thorpe's arrival?

Few humans living in the latter half of the twentieth century will ever know the thrill of discovering a place on earth that has never been seen before. It is an experience that touches upon something ancient and universal within the individual, and one feels bestowed with a kind of natural honor.

Honored. That is how Thorpe felt at this moment. Somehow, just by knowing he was the first soul to gaze over this great, enclosed canyon, he had the edifying sense that his whole life had been redeemed. At the moment his only regret was that Riley was not there to share the discovery. Good old Riley, he thought. One could not hope for a more loyal friend. He would have loved exploring this cavern . . . and I would have loved exploring it with him.

Slowly, yet steadily and surely, Thorpe's elation began to fade. He had a problem that demanded solving, and to do so he returned to a more pragmatic state of mind. The hole through which his head was poking was at least seventy feet above the cavern floor. He considered trying to retrieve the rope from the shaft, but he knew it would be difficult, if not impossible, to secure more than a twenty-foot length.

He dismissed the idea. Twenty feet would not solve the problem.

Finally he persuaded himself: "Forget the rope. You're going to have to climb down. If you are meant to make it, you will. Otherwise, good-bye, Thorpe. It was damn nice knowing you."

The time for hesitation was gone. He jammed the flashlight in the front of his pants, and then— cut, bruised, hands aching, alone, hungry, and frightened—he pulled himself through the opening and dug his toes and fingers into minute niches in the steep, rugged wall. *Caution* was the word of the moment, and in keeping with the word, Thorpe measured his ensuing descent in increments of iotas and inches.

As Thorpe was working his way into the infernal chasm, Riley was sitting in his hospital bed watching a spider climb down the wall. The spider meant nothing to him; he just happened to be watching the wall when the creature entered his field of view.

The door to his room opened and Lisette appeared. "I was sent to cheer you up. Pa-Preston said he'd give me ten dollars if I could make you smile."

Riley eyed Lisette with apathetic disregard.

"I'll split it with you."

Riley frowned and turned to glare out of the win-

dow. It was late in the afternoon on a hot, muggy
Monday, and the sun was all but hidden behind an
ugly gray haze.

Lisette could see Riley would not be easily humored. She moved a chair to the foot of the bed,
then sat down and openly examined her brother.
Aside from the obvious dour cast to his mouth, there
were deep lines of loss underscoring his pale blue
eyes. They looked like pools of pure pity, and they
told Lisette that her brother's misery was caused by
more than his physical inflictions. In fact, she was
fast developing a theory about the actual source of his
grief. It was a highly speculative theory, based primarily on intuition, and it involved the boy who had
protected her by the river that day—the boy who
might have harbored the spirit of her guardian angel.
In her mind, Riley had all but confessed that he
knew the boy.

Lisette coughed to draw Riley's attention, then
asked, "Is there anything I can do for you? You know,
like maybe take a message to someone in the mountains?"

Riley turned and stared blankly at Lisette. He was
beyond the mood for argument or evasion. With a
voice cracking under the weight of his own words, he
told her, "I'm afraid it's too late for messages."

"Too late?" Lisette was instinctively alarmed.

Riley nodded. He knew Lisette knew a part of the truth, and as he stared at her pretty face, he was reminded of Thorpe's absorbing interest in her. Now the thought that they would never meet turned in his gut like a serrated knife.

Lisette jumped to her feet. As she regarded the concept of boy as guardian angel, the boy side of the equation suddenly emerged as her principal concern. "Why do you say it's too late?"

Reluctantly, at a whisper, Riley replied, "Because there's no one to receive a message. He's gone."

"Gone?" Lisette's voice rang with dread. "He moved?"

Riley shook his head to answer no. A tear welled from his left eye and slid down his cheek.

"Is he dead?" Lisette asked the unthinkable.

Riley licked at the tear as it hit his lips, then blinked and looked away.

"What?" Lisette said sharply. "Why won't you tell me?"

Riley's gaze fell to the floor.

"Answer me, Riley," demanded Lisette. "We should do something. If someone is hurt . . . You don't have any proof that anybody is dead. Come on, let me help you. Let me help *him*."

Slowly, Riley lifted his sad eyes to Lisette. "I don't have proof, but still, I know: There's no one out there to help."

Lisette refused to believe what her brother was implying. This was not supposed to be: Her guardian angel could not die. It would mean there was no mercy in the world if God took Riley's friend in the same summer that Alison and Russel were taken. It would mean that heaven had fallen down. "Riley, don't give up hope. Don't stop believing."

Thorpe was two-thirds of the way down when he felt the wall recede from his grasp. As he fell, the image of Riley flying his pup tent off of Bluff Top flashed through his head. Then he hit the cavern floor with a thump.

Time did not move within that vast, dark gallery. It simply existed.

Sixteen

Thorpe had no notion of how long he was out. It might have been an hour; it might have been ten. He just knew that it hurt to breathe. With his mind he traveled slowly over his body. Every square inch of it seemed to ache simultaneously. Fortunately, he was still in one piece. Except for the boil on the back of his neck, which had been lacerated along the way and was now oozing freely, nothing was broken.

There was no need to move. Not yet. It seemed perfectly reasonable just to remain on the cavern floor, where time was marked by centuries, rather than days or weeks or months or years. It was enough just to lie there and hold on to the thin thread of being that pulsated ever so lightly in his chest.

It was thirst that eventually lifted him to his feet and sent him wandering through a seemingly infinite maze of corridors and shallow ditches. By this point he was resigned to his initial, fatal analysis of the situation, but the body has its own propensity for living, and the body's survival depends on water. Indeed, if it were not for his thirst, Thorpe would have been content to curl up in a ball and greet the Old Maker.

He knew there was water somewhere. He could feel it in the cool dampness that hung in the air. Vaguely, faintly, he thought he could hear water trickling on the far side of the cavern. Or was it an audible delusion? A wishful projection of a weary mind?

He used the flashlight sparingly, knowing that when it went he would become a blind man stumbling through an obstacle course. Although he lacked a comprehensive image of the cavern and had no clear idea of where he stood in the midst of it all, he detected a slight slope to the terrain, and he used that as a guide. Water, he knew, always sought the lowest level.

He went into corridors that ended in rooms that led nowhere. He followed ditches into pits. He circumambulated large mounds. He narrowly avoided stepping into chasms. He backed away from high barriers, climbed over boulders, and tripped forward over loose stones.

He was too exhausted to despair. Thirst kept him moving, while the gradual fall of the cavern drew him ever westward. Though he did not realize it at

the time, he was traveling through the heart and soul
of Bluff Top Ridge.

On Tuesday Doctor Kimmel decided that Riley was
sufficiently recovered from his concussion and released him from the hospital. Exactly a week before,
everyone in Bluff County had been bracing themselves for Camille's arrival. Now many of them—not
the least of whom was Riley—were dealing with the
stark repercussions of that wanton monster.

Because of the heavy cast on Riley's leg, Clara
moved a bed into her ground-floor sewing room and
installed him there. She did not understand why he
was still in such a surly mood, but he was, and she
did not try to cheer him up. Her grandmotherly response was to treat him with solicitous and acquies-
cent tenderness.

The sewing room had a window that faced east,
opening onto the front porch. As Riley sat propped
up in bed, gazing languidly over the north end of the
Sparkling River Valley, he was grateful that he could
not see the bold shape of Bluff Top Ridge. If he had
his druthers, he would never set eyes on that cursed
mountain again.

He would not read. He would not allow visitors.
He just sat there grappling with remorse.

On a table by the bed was a photograph of his
mother and father. They stood hand in hand by the

Sparkling River. Alison was beaming her trademark smile, while Russel was wearing the subtle smirk of someone who knew a great secret. Riley studied the photograph with a kind of baffled detachment. For all his life he had thought of them as parents; people whose job it was to feed and shelter him. But now he saw them as the individuals they once were: people, just like him . . . people whose dreams were dashed and taken away. The perception was too terrible to bear. "God," he exclaimed at the photograph. "I miss you. I wish we'd known each other longer. But listen, soon a friend of mine is going to be joining you, and I'd like it if you'd make him feel welcome. His name is Thorpe, and he's had a tough, tough time."

With that, Riley reached over and lay the photograph flat on the table. Suddenly it was clear to him what he had to do. And so, as twilight was settling over the Blue Ridge Mountains, he began in his mind to compose a letter. *Dear Nina Greenwood, Probably you remember me. I'm sure you do. I was Thorpe's blood brother before he . . . Dear Nina, I am sorry to have to tell you this, but . . . Dear Nina Greenwood, I know from the way he talked about you that Thorpe loved you, but now he is . . . gone.*

Thorpe might have looked gone, but he was not gone yet. After stumbling forward for hours, he had eventually zeroed in on the sibilant sound of falling water and followed it to its elusive source. Hidden under the towering west wall of the cavern was a shallow stream running through a groove that time and soft persistence had carved in a bed of solid rock. Now he was lying motionless in that groove, receiving the cool, life-sustaining ablutions of the precious water.

Several feet ahead of where Thorpe lay, the bed of rock ended abruptly and the stream plummeted into a deep, dark hole. He could hear the water splashing into a turbulent pool below. The sound was entrancing. It washed through him like euphonic chamber music and kept the dire reality of his circumstances at bay.

Hours passed, yet Thorpe felt no motivation to move from that smooth channel in the rock. He cared only to listen to his babbling friend, the waterfall.

Eventually he noticed that he no longer felt hungry. It was almost as if his body had gotten tired of crying for nourishment. Now, finally, he accepted that the great drama of his life had come to its final act. He had accomplished his last mission. He had found water. There was nothing more he could think to ask of himself.

So, he thought calmly, that's that.

He lifted himself up on his knees and took the flashlight off the ledge where he had placed it earlier.

Then he crawled forward to the edge of the hole and sat with his legs dangling in the waterfall. He withdrew Lisette's necklace from his pocket, flicked open the locket, and read aloud the inscription. *Such is our love that even the angels in heaven are impressed.*

He placed the necklace over his head, threw the flashlight over his shoulder, and jumped.

Thorpe knew it was an irrevocable act, and as he sank helplessly through the air, he cried out, "Someone open those pearly gates!"

It was an involuntary physical reaction that caused him to flail at the churning surface of the pool and gasp for air. It was a similar kind of corporeal instinct that had him hold his breath as a truculent current pulled his ravaged body down and under.

Thorpe did not fight the force that had him. He let it sweep him blindly and swiftly along. He crossed his arms over his chest and projected his legs in a stiff line. He had about as much control over his movement as a bit of flotsam riding a storm-wracked sea. He rotated and spiraled. He glanced off rock. His feet jammed in a recess and he was spun around.

His lungs were about to burst when the current suddenly abated and he felt himself rising. The ride was over. He bobbed to the surface and gasped for air.

It took him a moment to realize he was standing on a soft bottom. He floundered in the darkness until

he bumped against land, then flopped backward onto
the firmament. Just as he was retreating into uncon-
sciousness, he saw a plenitude of pinpoint lights.
They looked like stars twinkling in a huge dome. Am
I dreaming already, he wondered, or is this the face of
my death?

Seventeen

As was her habit, Phyllis Applegate took her morning cup of hot tea with her as she strolled to the bubbling springs. The cup fell instantly from her hand when she saw the battered boy sprawled on the ground beside the gazebo.

For all of Phyllis's adult life she had wanted a child to nurture and protect, and as she rushed to Thorpe's side, she had already begun to pray that he continued to breathe. She fell to her knees and hunched over him like a supplicant nun.

Yes. There was warmth. There was a systole of breath.

She tore herself away and scrambled toward the house calling for her husband, "Eunice! Eunice!"

The judge was in the kitchen, still wearing his bathrobe. He shuffled to an open window and inquired, "Yes, dear?"

"Come faster than you can come to the springs."

"What?"

"Come," Phyllis commanded. Then she turned and raced to the destitute soul lying on the ground at the foot of the ridge.

When the retired Judge Applegate arrived, he found his wife holding Thorpe's head in her lap and praying.

The old couple carefully lifted the nearly lifeless boy and carted him back along the path to the house. The judge had a hunch that this was the Greenwood boy, who had been missing for so long from neighboring High County, but he did not say anything to that effect. Instead he whispered repeatedly, "You're going to be all right, son. You're going to be all right."

Phyllis also had a hunch about the identity of the gaunt youngster she had found. Her intuition was confirmed when she saw the gold chain and locket hanging from his neck. After placing him in one of the guest-room beds, she reverently removed the necklace from around his neck and hung it on a bedpost.

With the judge scurrying to assist at her slightest beck and bid, Phyllis ran to the kitchen pantry, grabbed a clutch of dried comfrey, and began preparing a poultice. While she waited for the water to boil, she withdrew a container of beef broth from the re-

frigerator and started it to simmering on the stove.
As soon as the comfrey was ready, she raced back to
the guest room and put the warm, emulsified plant
directly onto the lacerated boil on Thorpe's neck. Afterward she wrapped the wound with gauze and began
to wash and disinfect his numerous other cuts and
scrapes. When this was done, she lovingly applied a
salve to each and every small abrasion.

All of Phyllis's ministrations were done with the
utmost tenderness, and as she performed them, she silently prayed; she was trying hard not to disturb the
dear boy's sleep.

The judge entered as Phyllis was combing Thorpe's
ash-black hair. He was bearing the broth in a bowl
with a wooden spoon. "Yes, dear?" he inquired tim-
idly. "What should I do with this?"

"Give it to me," Phyllis replied. "Then go around
and sit on the other side of the bed. We're going to
have to jostle him up so I can spoon this nutrition
into his system."

"Yes, dear."

Weakly, and completely unconscious of what he
was doing, Thorpe resisted the Applegates' benevo-
lent efforts.

"Sit behind him, Eunice," Phyllis instructed.
"Hold him against your chest. I need to concentrate
on spooning."

Eunice Applegate nodded to his wife, then climbed onto the bed and enclasped Thorpe in a gentle bear hug. The physical act of holding the weak, defenseless runaway stirred up deep emotions in the old judge. His voice was low and grave as he sought to reassure Thorpe. "You're going to be all right, son. You're going to be all right."

Phyllis grabbed Thorpe's jaw and held it with just enough firmness to overcome his faint resistance. After spilling much of the first spoonful down his chin, she managed to ply a full serving into his mouth. Hardly conscious of what he was doing, he smacked his lips and swallowed. He was more receptive to the next spoonful, and then, by the third, he became an eager participant in the activity. Phyllis was tickled by her success. She smiled lovingly at her husband and giggled. "He's taking it now, Eunice. He wants more."

"He's obviously famished," noted the judge. "I only hope we found him in time."

Phyllis was overjoyed as Thorpe slurped greedily at the next spoonful of broth. In her delight she beamed at her husband. "Oh, Eunice, you're such a good man for caring."

The judge dipped his head and blushed.

Phyllis continued with her efforts until the bowl was empty. Then she and Eunice carefully lay the weary Thorpe Greenwood down amongst a collection of pillows. "Oh, the poor, poor boy," she mused. "Lord knows what he's been through."

"I can't imagine," said the judge, shaking his head as he arose from the bed. He stood back a step and eyed the scene with a concerned expression. After a moment he cleared his throat and announced, "I'll call for an ambulance."

Phyllis shot a sharp glance at her husband. "No, Eunice."

"No? What do you mean, no?" The judge was taken aback.

"I mean, don't call an ambulance," Phyllis said clearly. "I found him, I'm going to keep him."

"You . . . ah, sweetheart, you can't keep him."

Phyllis chose to ignore her husband. Gently, she adjusted the covers over Thorpe's sleeping form.

Old Judge Applegate hemmed unhappily. "Phyllis, dear, the boy is thin as a rail. He needs immediate medical attention."

Phyllis shook her head in disagreement, then gave her husband an imploring look. "He's all right medically. He's just hungry and weak. What he needs now is tender, loving care."

"Sweetheart." Eunice Applegate shifted from foot to foot. "I'm certain that is the missing Greenwood boy from High County. Legally, I'm bound to report his presence here. Besides . . ."

"Besides what?" Phyllis asked pointedly.

"Well . . ." He paused. "We'd be responsible if . . ."

"If what?"

Eunice Applegate was cowed by Phyllis's sharp tone. He did not think she was behaving rationally. He addressed her in a soft voice. "We'd be responsible if his condition deteriorated."

Phyllis carefully adjusted the pillow beneath Thorpe's head and then stood up slowly from the bed. She gazed willfully at her husband and explained, "Eunice, this boy came to me for a special reason. He is Lisette Sutter's guardian angel. I am the one who told her he existed, and I am the one meant to resuscitate him."

The judge frowned. Several arguments formed in his mind, but something about his wife's sure manner made him hold his tongue. Many years of living with the woman had taught him that she was rarely wrong when she asserted herself as she was doing now.

Phyllis could see by her husband's hesitancy that she was winning him over. "All that aside, Eunice, it would be unwise to move him now. Let me keep him for a few days."

The judge frowned again, yet nodded his assent. "As you say, dear. But you have to promise you'll let me call a doctor if he takes a turn for the worse."

"I promise."

It had been a long day for the Applegates.

Phyllis sent Eunice to his own room to get a good night's sleep, then ensconced herself in the chair by Thorpe's bed and kept a tireless vigil through the night. In her heart she prayed, *Lord, bring this boy around.*

At dawn when Thorpe awoke in a disoriented stupor, she soothed him with the soft words "Son, whoever you are, you made it through. Whoever you are, you're safe now."

Thorpe looked at Phyllis with an uncomprehending expression, mumbled something unintelligible, then fell back into the healing world of sleep. A few minutes later when he awoke again, she was waiting with a bowl of stewed apricots and oatmeal. This time he worked in concert with his hunger, leaning forward to receive the gift of food.

As Thorpe ate he eyed his benefactress with the appreciative curiosity of a helpless animal. He had not yet figured out where he was, or why, or how he had gotten there, but he understood his luck had changed.

Phyllis was still in her chair at noon when Thorpe awoke for the third time that day. He looked at her with a weak yet urgent expression on his face and said, "Bathroom."

Phyllis was ecstatic. She took it as a very good sign that Thorpe was able to express his needs, and even

a better sign that he was able to climb from the bed
with minimal assistance. Although he tottered at first
when his feet hit the floor, he managed to steady himself and take a few steps. She now knew her prayers
had been answered; the boy was coming around.

While Thorpe was occupied in the bathroom,
Phyllis ran to the kitchen, where she concocted another comfrey poultice. The judge was in
Waynesboro, purchasing the articles of clothing and
other supplies that Phyllis had requested.

Thorpe was at first shocked, then mesmerized by
the gaunt face staring back at him in the bathroom
mirror. For a long while he just stood looking at his
own reflection, wondering who the strange individual
might be. Finally he understood: That's me. I went
through the mountain and I came out alive. Now I
can see Mom again. I can thank Riley. And God
bless me, if I'm lucky, I'll get to hear Lisette sing
again.

"Hallelujah!"

Phyllis had returned from the kitchen, and her
heart leapt at the sound of Thorpe's exultant cry.

A second later the bathroom door opened.
"Hello," Thorpe said shyly. He crossed the room and
sat in the chair by the bed. He was still feeble, but he
had regained full consciousness and there was a flush
of color in his cheeks.

Phyllis beamed joyously. "Hello."

"Thank you for saving me," Thorpe said politely, his voice rich with unaffected gratitude.

"You're welcome." Phyllis nodded. "Although I believe you saved yourself. All I did was wash and feed you."

Thorpe looked curiously at Phyllis for a moment and then asked, "Are you the woman that sits in the little building by the springs?"

"Yes, I am." Phyllis smiled, and then without a word of explanation, she moved behind Thorpe and started unraveling the gauze from his neck. He did not resist.

"How long have I been here?"

"A day and a half. We found you yesterday."

"Oh," said Thorpe, and then his thoughts drifted away on a stream of reminiscences.

After changing the gauze, Phyllis returned to the kitchen and retrieved the macaroni casserole she had left warming in the oven. Thorpe accepted the dish with an eager gleam in his eye, then made it quickly disappear in a frenzied attack. Afterward he downed a tall glass of cold milk in a single gulp.

When the food hit the bottom of Thorpe's shrunken stomach, he groaned. Then he burped, smiled apologetically, and flopped back in bed. Soon he was asleep again.

• • •

In the early evening when he awoke, he saw a new outfit of clothes folded neatly upon the chair beside the bed. On the floor by the chair was a pair of blue tennis shoes. In each shoe was a clean white sock. The thought of clean socks tickled him; he had almost forgotten the joy of dry feet. He sat up and stretched. On a nearby night table was a note: *Please, if you wish, join my husband and me for dinner. Perhaps you would enjoy a hot bath beforehand. Towels and soap by the tub. The toothbrush is for you. I will check in at seven.*

The note was signed, *The woman who sits by the springs*.

As Thorpe luxuriated in a hot bath, he wondered about the kind woman who was working so hard to help him. Although she had not introduced herself, nor asked his name, he had figured out that he was in the Applegates' home, and that the woman must be Mrs. Applegate. He remembered now that Riley had said she was a nice person, a spiritual, and a friend of Lisette's.

After dressing (the pants were a bit large in the waist, but the shoes fit perfectly), he took the necklace from the bedpost and hung it around his neck. Then he returned to the bathroom mirror and marveled for a long moment at his reflection.

My, he thought, I've changed.

He was in the hallway, wandering toward the center of the house, when he spotted the judge. "There you are, son," Eunice Applegate said, smiling warmly. "I was just coming to see if you would be joining us for dinner."

"Yes. Thank you," Thorpe said shyly.

Thorpe followed the judge onto the stoop leading down into the courtyard. Phyllis was waiting for them at the table. She cooed proudly when she saw the clean, well-dressed guest. "Well, don't you look healthy and handsome."

"Much improved from yesterday," decreed the judge.

"Thank you," Thorpe said respectfully. He felt a warm rush of gratitude toward his saviors. Suddenly, it became clear to him that he was going to take them into his confidence and reveal the truth about himself. "I, ah ... appreciate all you've done."

"Oh, you're so polite." Phyllis beamed at Thorpe. "We only did what any decent souls would do. Come, let's eat."

Thorpe's appetite was voracious. He consumed three glasses of milk, four rolls, two fried chicken thighs, two baked potatoes, and several servings of green beans.

"I hope you've saved room for dessert."

"Afraid I'm full," Thorpe said with a burp, then blushed with embarrassment. "Excuse me."

"That's fine at this table." The judge chuckled tolerantly.

"It means he's full," noted Phyllis.

Thorpe suppressed another burp before remarking, "That was the tastiest meal I've had in ages."

Thorpe Greenwood was as charmed by the Applegates as Riley and Lisette had been. During the hour after dinner he spoke openly and freely about himself. Prompted only by a timely question or two, he recounted for his hosts the unlikely events that had driven him from home and caused him to reside for over a year in the shadows of Bluff Top. Some of his tale the Applegates already knew, or had partially imagined, while other parts of it left them quite astonished. Phyllis shed tears when he told of his journey into the bowels of the mountain.

When he finished speaking, he felt relieved of a great emotional burden, yet physically, the effort left him exhausted.

His weariness was obvious to Phyllis. "You go right on back to bed, my daring young man. Tomorrow if you feel up to it, we'll pay the Sutters a visit."

"Thank you so much." Thorpe yawned as he stood.

"Thorpe."

"Yes, sir?"

Eunice Applegate stood, and in a voice filled with empathy and warmth, he assured the weary youngster, "Don't worry any more about your troubles. In the morning I'm going to drive to Richmond and visit my old friend the governor. We were like blood brothers once. I believe the two of us can make certain arrangements to suit you and your mother."

Thorpe's deep blue eyes sparkled with moisture as he looked upon the kindly old judge. "I can't thank you enough, sir."

The judge was suddenly choked with emotion. He took a moment to fight back the moisture in his own eyes, then opened his arms and offered, "This is your home for the time being. You just plan on staying here with us until we get things straightened out."

Thorpe too was overwhelmed with emotion. He could not speak.

Phyllis looked proudly at her husband, then arose and took Thorpe by the arm. Gracefully and gently, she ushered him toward the house. "You go sleep. You deserve all the rest this world will let you get."

Eighteen

Thorpe slept the sweet sleep of a satiated cat. In the morning when he awoke a broad smile spread over his thin face. The bed was soft. The pillows were clean and comfy. There was the promise of a hot breakfast. This was better than a dream.

Finally, after so much hardship, life had begun to work in his favor again.

He lay studying the stucco ceiling, anticipating the coming day. He had heard from Phyllis about Riley's accident at the foot of Gallihugh Mountain, and he presumed his blood brother knew about the landslide that had blocked the cave entrance. Won't Riley be surprised to see me! The idea that he would soon see his partner again sent a rush of joy tingling through his bones.

Then suddenly it hit Thorpe that he would soon

hear news of his mother. His apprehension at the thought put a mental damper on his joy.

He got up and slipped on his new blue tennis shoes. He took the necklace from his neck and stuffed it in a pocket. The prospect of meeting Lisette face to face—of looking directly in her eyes—aroused an emotion in him that was too dynamic and too exhilarating to name or comprehend.

Phyllis served poached eggs, banana pancakes, and freshly squeezed orange juice for breakfast. Thorpe and the judge sat across from each other at the small kitchen table. Both were too busy eating to engage in conversation. When the meal was over, the judge poured a hot cup of coffee, then excused himself from the table. "Y'all have a nice day," he said, nodding to Thorpe and Phyllis. "I'm off to Richmond to twist the governor's ear."

While Thorpe waited alone at the table, Phyllis washed and put away the dishes, then picked up the phone and called Clara Sutter. "I'm coming there shortly with a friend," she said.

Phyllis drove south around the end of Bluff Top Ridge, proceeded east over the range of hills at Jagged Gap, then turned north into the Sparkling River Valley. To fill the silence, she explained her husband's mission to Thorpe. "You shouldn't get your hopes up too high—these things take time—but the judge believes he might be able to arrange to have your mother released soon."

As Thorpe sat quietly in the passenger seat and admired the undulating beauty of the surrounding mountains, it was already difficult for him to believe he had survived for so long in those vast and ancient woods.

Meanwhile, up ahead at the Upper Place, Riley was feeling bleak. He was depressed. He felt hollow inside. His outlook was pessimistic. His mood was dismal and blue. He was despondent. He felt alone, dejected, embittered, and sad.

Actually, there is no way to accurately describe Riley's state of mind as he sat in his grandmother's sewing room on the morning of August 30, 1969. His parents remained only as a photograph on a table. His left leg was broken. His blood brother had been sealed alive inside of a solution cave. It was his duty to inform Nina Greenwood of her son's tragic demise.

Let's just say Riley was not in a receptive mood when he heard the sound of a vehicle coming up the driveway. A glance out the window informed him it was one of the Applegates' cars. "No. Not now," he moaned. "I hope they aren't coming to see me."

Lisette and Kissy were lounging in Lisette's bedroom when Kissy looked through the east window and saw the car. "I believe it's Mrs. Applegate," she said.

"Great," exclaimed Lisette. She jumped from her chair and prepared to dash downstairs, then halted in her tracks when Kissy observed, "Hey, there's someone with her. A skinny, dark-headed guy. He looks our age."

Lisette and Kissy kneeled in the shadows by the second-floor banister and watched quietly as Clara and Preston greeted the visitors in the foyer. Although Lisette was unable to get a good look at the dark-haired boy's face, she knew it was none other than Riley's secret friend, her protector.

"Let's go down," whispered Kissy.

"Are you crazy?"

"Lisette, you're trembling."

"I know I'm trembling. So what?"

Preston pointed the mystery boy toward the sewing room door, then followed Clara and Phyllis into the den.

"Come on." Lisette started to tiptoe down the stairs.

"Where are you going?"

"To the garden. I need to compose myself."

"Are you all right?"

"Yes. No. Oh, come on, Kissy."

"What?" Riley replied sourly to the knock on his door. After the knock was repeated, he grumbled, "I said, what?"

The door swung open and Thorpe Greenwood sauntered into the room. "Hi, Riley. Heard you had an accident. Thought I'd drop by for a visit."

Riley did a double take. His heart saw the truth before his mind could tolerate the fact. It was as if the entire universe had changed direction before his eyes. "Thorpe! It's you. My God!" he screamed. "You're alive!"

"Yep," Thorpe chortled with abandon. "I'm alive, and let me tell you, it wasn't an accident."

Riley's jaw fell open with incredulity.

Thorpe grinned as he watched Riley absorb the reality of his resurrection.

Riley shut his eyes. And then when he opened them again and Thorpe was still standing there, he whispered, "Thorpe, you bastard. You amazing bastard. I never thought I'd see you again."

Thorpe stepped forward with an extended hand. "Put it there. Don't worry, I'm not a ghost."

Riley clasped Thorpe's hand and cried, "This whole time I thought the landslide had you trapped in your cave. I thought you were a goner, man. I thought you were dead."

"I was trapped," Thorpe said as he continued to pump Riley's hand. "And for a while there, I thought I was a goner, too."

"Wow! Man! Really?"

"Yeah. Really."

"What happened?"

Thorpe released Riley's hand and sat down on the end of the bed. "I'll tell you in a minute. But first, how are you? This is a pretty serious-looking cast on your leg."

Riley scoffed at his cast as if it were a minor annoyance. "Broken femur and a cracked shin. It's nothing. The doctor says I'll be up and around in a month or so. I'm better now that you're here."

"I'm better now that I'm here, too." Thorpe grinned with amusement. "I missed you, man. Haven't seen you since Mark Rawlings left to catch the bus to Petersburg."

"Oh, yeah," Riley cried excitedly. "Your mother was cool, and guess what!"

"What?"

"Your worries are over. You're free. Your mom divorced that guy Harry."

"Do what?"

As Thorpe and Riley sat in the sewing room discussing the significant happenings of the past several weeks, Lisette sat on the chestnut bench and stared wide-eyed at her shimmering reflection. She was not sure why she felt so giddy, but giddy she felt indeed. It was as if ten monarch butterflies had emerged from a chrysalis in her stomach.

"They're still in there talking," reported Kissy as she popped through the arbored entrance.

"Thanks," said Lisette. "Now go back and keep an eye on them. Let me know when he comes out."

Kissy saluted, then returned to her observation post behind a bush at the end of the porch.

Lisette's gaze did not waver from the face dancing upon the surface of the pool. As she continued to stare, the water grew strangely still, until soon she could see her reflection as surely as if she were looking in a mirror. This newly clear image of herself helped to calm her and restore her inner balance. *Yes,* she thought, *I believe, and believing brought my angel to me.* This is the way it's supposed to be.

Kissy suddenly appeared at the garden entrance and called excitedly to Lisette, "Get ready, he's coming. I told him you were out here."

"You told him?!" Lisette stood, then immediately sat back down. "Kissy, don't leave."

"Bye, Lisette." Kissy giggled musically as she darted away.

Lisette was looking straight through her reflection when she heard the crunch of footsteps on the gravel path leading through the garden to the chestnut bench. The steps were tentative. They stopped several yards behind the bench.

Lisette turned slowly.

"Lisette?"

"Yes."

"Hello. My name is Thorpe."

"Hi," she squeaked, then smiled warmly.

Thorpe blushed. It was evident that he wanted to speak, yet no words seemed willing to come.

Realizing that he was more nervous than she, Lisette stood and motioned at the bench. "Thorpe, would you like to join me?"

Thorpe nodded yes and stepped forward. But he halted at the edge of the pool and reached into a pocket. There was an earnest look of friendship in his eyes as he stammered, "I have something to give you."

"Oh?"

"Yes. It's something you left by the river one day. I've been keeping it safe until I had the chance to return it to you in person."

When Lisette saw Thorpe draw her mother's necklace from his pocket, she made a sound that was part gasp, part sigh, and part happy moan.

A bioelectric spark shot from Thorpe's hand to Lisette's hand as she accepted the locket. Then, in an abrupt forward movement, with warmth and affection emanating from her whole being, Lisette traveled the fifty inches to where Thorpe was standing beside the pool. She threw her arms around his shoulders. It was by instinct that his arms wrapped around her trim waist. "Thank you for this, Thorpe," she gushed. "You're an angel."

Thorpe wanted to say, "And you better believe I'm impressed." But all he could do was stand there and hold on to the dream that was hugging him.

And although it meant little or nothing to them, as Lisette and Thorpe embraced, the ancient mountains laughed. In all their hundreds of millions of years they had never witnessed a more satisfying moment in time.

About the Author

Sid Hite grew up in Bowling Green, Virginia. After leaving high school he traveled for several years through Europe, Asia, and South America before returning to Virginia and the Blue Ridge Mountains.

He is the author of *Dither Farm*, which the *Boston Sunday Globe* hailed as "one of the funniest, most heartwarming books of the year." He lives in Sag Harbor, New York.